Michael Gills

Burning Down
My Father's House

ALSO BY MICHAEL GILLS

Novels

Before All Who Have Ever Seen This Disappear
The Go Love Quartet: Emergency Instructions
Go Love
West
New Harmony

Short Stories

Burning Down My Father's House
The House Across from the Deaf School
The Death of Bonnie and Clyde and other Stories
Why I Lie

Essays

Finisterre: Book Two of White Indians
White Indians

Praise for Michael Gills

"Michael Gills's *Why I Lie* is one of the most intense experiences I have ever encountered. Every page is vivid with life, livid with truth. The author has discovered a style with which to fashion the darkest of hours into fierce explosions of light. His pages shudder and throb. This book is unique, invaluable, not to be missed."

— Fred Chappell, author of *I Am One of You Forever*

"These stories are, scene by scene, sentence by sentence, beautifully written—clean, gorgeous prose, perfectly pitched. The detail work is exquisite. Michael Gills gives us deep blood ties and profound betrayals. He understands both the need to belong and the drive to escape. Suffering and loss are given their necessary place in these stories, but so too are grace and mercy. Buy this book. Read it. You'll be glad you did."

— Donald Hays, author of *The Dixie Association*

"What a wallop these ten stories pack. Michael Gills is the real thing—a storyteller whose sentences make you want to clap with Saturday night's hullabaloo and Sunday morning's holiness. Unstopper the bourbon reserved for honored guests when you read *Why I Lie*, which is a potent distillation unto itself."

— Dale Ray Phillips, author of *My People's Waltz*

"Michael Gills's book is an original composition—while paying homage to the Southern fiction and poetry it comes from. It will grind you fine. It will trouble your heart."

— James Whitehead, author of *Joiner*

"Jack, Louisa, and the characters of *Why I Lie* eat roadkill, Slim Jim's, stay dead broke, travel on, and speak out of a briarpatch of curses and poetry. Michael Gills's prose reeks with accuracy and bulls-eye intensity and these interlocking stories are a thrilling good read."

— William Harrison, author of *Black August*

"Michael Gills gives us a world writ large, a world where gods and heraldic beasts step full-blown to live among us. His is a world of big hurts—of broken jaws and heads, broken checkbooks and broken hearts—but it is a world of even greater acts of contrition and forgiveness. His people dance, sing, and pray to stay alive—after all, they are Southern people. If stories are lies that tell the truth, then this collection is filled with whoppers."

— Jim Clark, editor, *The Greensboro Review*

"It doesn't matter if Michael Gills's hellbent and dream-filled characters populate the backwoods of Arkansas or the wide-open shorelines of North Carolina—each one shows more soul than a wagonload of do-gooders. This handful of great stories displays what all good country songs prove. People stuck Here want to be Elsewhere, and people Elsewhere want to be Home. *The Death of Bonnie and Clyde* is one beautiful ring with eleven separate, perfect gemstones displayed."

— George Singleton, author of *The Half-Mammals of Dixie*

"This beautiful book of stories is more constellation than collection: it radiates like a great old myth, and carries us along with a novel's momentum, and a lyrical, sensual voice. Michael Gills's young lovers build their fragile new lives in the shadow of old family violence and the fleeting beauty of an ever-surprising Southern landscape."

— Marjorie Sandor, author of The *Secret Music of Tordesillas*

"Gills's beautifully written prose...combines his warring natures—the daring macho infused crazy man with the earth-reverent husband and father. This book is a reminder that we Americans still live on a continent that recently was a wilderness, and that we all possess an atavistic need to interact with it. For those of us not so good as Michael Gills at camping, hiking and white-water rafting, he's offered us a thrilling armchair version."

— Diane Wakowski, author of *The Diamond Dog*

Contents

Library of Congress Cataloging-in-Publication Data

Names: Gills, Michael, 1960- author.
Title: Burning down my Father's house : stories / Michael Gills.
Description: First edition. | Hunstville, Texas : TRP: The University Press
    of SHSU, [2023]
Identifiers: LCCN 2023014175 (print) | LCCN 2023014176 (ebook) | ISBN
    9781680033137 (paperback) | ISBN 9781680033144 (ebook)
Subjects: LCSH: Families—Southern States—Fiction. | LCGFT: Domestic
    fiction. | Short stories.
Classification: LCC PS3607.I45 B87 2023 (print) | LCC PS3607.I45 (ebook)
    | DDC 813/.6—dc23/eng/20230426
LC record available at https://lccn.loc.gov/2023014175
LC ebook record available at https://lccn.loc.gov/2023014176

FIRST EDITION
Front cover image courtesy: Shutterstock
Author photo courtesy: Jeff Hanson/University of Utah

Cover design by Bradley Alan Ivey
Interior design by Bradley Alan Ivey

Printed and bound in the United States of America

TRP: The University Press of SHSU
Huntsville, Texas 77341
texasreviewpress.org

Grateful acknowledgement and thanks to the editors of the following journals where these stories originally appeared: "Emergency Instructions," *The Texas Review,* ed., Eric Miles Williamson; "What the Newly Dead Don't Know But Learn," *Industrial Works of the World,* ed., William Hastings, and, in another form, *Night Train,* Rusty Barnes; "A Funeral For The Living" and "Yonder," *Goliad,* ed., Joe Haske and Dan Mendoza; "Swimmer," *South Carolina Review;* ed. Keith Lee Morris; "Burning Down My Father's House," *Tough,* ed. Rusty Barnes; "Sebastian Rising," *Kestrel,* ed., Donna Long and Suzanne Heagy.

All thanks and love to my wife and daughter, without whom none of this work would happen.

for James Steven Gills

BURNING DOWN MY FATHER'S HOUSE

Stories

Michael Gills

TRP: The University Press of SHSU
Huntsville, Texas 77341

Emergency Instructions

An unforecast rain had flooded the basement, so Joey'd had to climb through the trap door into the crawl space dragging a utility light on an orange extension cord that was plugged into a light socket above the muddy waterline. He'd hardwired the electric pump after it became clear that their realtor was a deceitful cocksucker who'd concealed the ranch house's history of flood. Now it flashed through his mind that he could die down there ankle-deep, fumbling with the monkey-rigged switch while mice skittered in the dark from which the poison-stoned bug sprayer man had once dragged a hog-nose snake, little strips of silvery skin flaying off its back. "This'n won't bother you," he'd said, and Joey'd found it out front, looped in the fork of a dogwood.

November, a warm trough had sailed up from the gulf, colliding with the first brace of cold from the Rockies, deer season, so the purple-painted fence posts glowed outside in the yellow light, and a troop of blaze orange hunters had tromped across the back pasture. Joey'd seen them behind the barn, ought-sixes and shotguns and lever-action .30-.30s in the crooks of their arms, and just as dark came, while what was left of the hickory leaves fell, a shot came from the wood and Joey recognized the sound of a slug hitting meat. A pile of field-dressed guts lay out there steaming. That's how it was on the cusp of the millennium, when they'd hauled off and moved back to Joey's native state. Renee imagined Hunter Man peeking through every window, the only neighbors a half-mile off sighting their rifles in off a fall-down front porch, just like some hayseed dream of the place, 333 Barton Road, Dover, Arkansas, first right before the curve—they'd bought the farm.

The pump kicked on, *omp-omping* out the basement window onto the green septic grass. It's a Tuesday, Joey's off day from ArkaTech where he taught American history, especially southern conflicts involving Mormons, to the offspring of Pope County, some of whom threatened to blow up his truck in hand-scrawled notes stuck with bits of juicy fruit to his office door in windowless fart-smelling Witherspoon Hall. He'd dug a trench to gather the seep, could see it glisten in the side footer where he pick-axed a hole from a flower bed straight down and patched the concrete, but not the leak. Outside, thunder, wind in the trees and the far of whacka-whack of a Pileated.

Joey knew his predicament—a kid who'd played wide receiver at Jackrabbit High'd died the same way. Should he somehow ground the little hook light and extension cord into the cold water, 110 volts would sear through his blood, and, without 220's kick, glue him to the spot, so no one would find him while he cooked through the day, not until Renee walked into one wing of the huge house, holding two-year-old Lara's hand and calling his name. "Joe?" she'd say. "Joker? Stop it." She'd search room to room to room. No Joe.

Odd. His truck was in its spot.

Eventually, she'd walk to the barn, turn the light on in the tack room where a roof rat had chewed through floorboard. She'd say his name, walk back out and circle the house, see the basement door ajar, hear the pump gurgle. Surely Lara'd be with her, holding her right hand, that sweet far-off look in her eyes—*where daddy?* They'd walk to the little trap door together, their footprints side by side. Renee would see him first. She'd reach without thinking—what did she know of current? The juice would pass from him into her, and that would be a surprise because she'd never felt it, that hot rippling. And little Lara'd reach to Mommy, *what wrong with Mommy?* and there they'd be, the three of them bound with no one in the world to throw the switch. What a goddamn mess.

Ankle-deep with a sump pump, Joey'd just thought—*goddamn mess*—when it happened. A tiny flash sizzled and popped. He held a breath, for some reason thought of collards he'd once planted in Carolina on top of whole fish carcasses. Through the various doors he'd crawled through came the horn blast, high and loud and true, as if all the dogs on earth had lifted snouts in a single howl. It was surely the same warning they'd had explained to them umpteen times when they signed papers, and again by the blue book. Fourteen miles south in R'ville, the siren signaled a problem at the reactor. Upstairs, in the pale blue manual titled EMERGENCY INSTRUCTIONS, are the bulleted directives on what to do at such a moment. Out the crawl door onto wet concrete and away from the valley of the shadow of death, he saw the light, the arc and square of it framed, and everything would be alright. Let the pump do its work. His mama, Josephine, was due to come stay for a weekend. There'd be cooking and laughter, and maybe he'd build the season's first fire. Thanksgiving was in the works—Renee's people were driving up from Florida so, for the first time since the wedding, both families would converge. The feast would be on and Joey'd carve the biggest goddamn turkey Price Chopper sold and Lara'd wear a brand new dress.

He left the basement, the alarm in his ears. Down Barton Road, the neighbor's walker dogs howled in sync with the siren, so the two sounds tangled and for the rest of his days Joey'd hear them mixed—a mutant symbol of his life until then.

Every number he punched was busy. Cow Jumped Over the Moon, *busy.* R'ville Middle, Room 14, *busy.* Principal Titsworth, *busy.* ArkaTech, *busy.* The big house ticked. It still smelled like the Elliotts, their hair in the carpet fiber, their sloughed skin down the sink drains, their shit filling half the septic tank.

Joey opened the drawer, took it in hand. The cover sketch was a hokey Nuclear One, computer generated. EMERGENCY INSTRUCTIONS, the thing said. EFFECTIVE *NOW.* Written on the sixth-grade level, the index broke the book into parts like "What Is An Emergency?" followed by "What Do I Do?" and "Do I Need Special Help?" "Are there deaf residents in my neighborhood?" the book asked in twenty point font, every letter bolded. "Go tell them." STAY CALM! Joey was instructed. DO NOT PANIC!

Joey opened the cedar armoire, switched on the stereo. Nothing but static. He kept his cool, stayed calm. The siren and its sister-dogs had shut up. Maybe it was a mistake, maybe he'd breathed too many fumes in the basement. It was Tuesday. What kind of a day was Tuesday for a meltdown? That'd be a Friday night sort of thing, or Sunday morning with all the church bells clanging. But Tuesday? *Monday* would be better than Tuesday, no matter what Lynyrd Skynyrd said. Tuesday was lame. But it was Tuesday, November 16, 1999, in Pope County, Arkansas—the Leonid meteors tonight, no doubt about it.

Renee was in her classroom at Russellville Middle, about to unwrap a turkey on wheat, stare out at ArkaTech's shining white cupola and wonder how she got mixed up in all this. Lara's at Cow Jumped Over The Moon, where they have *hot-hot* drills to practice for this very day. Joey thought of all the people he'd ever loved that had died. He didn't know why. What would it be like to be dead and not know that your people were about to be radiated to kingdom come, their wails rising in a crescendo beyond any siren or Walker Dog? Would the dead know of such a moment? Would deep silence revive their listening?

In the great room, Moondog saws logs. Last night's storm kept her up all night. She's been scared of thunder since a puppy back in North Carolina when Hugo blew through Greensboro and knocked all the trees down on the college golf course. They'd burned slick-barked logs carved with names of lovers for three whole winters.

The siren again.

The front porch faced a hickory treed acre where wild turkey and whitetail traipsed past the well-house with a skiff of frost on it just now, the *thump-thump* from the Ajax gas well like Aztec drumbeat through the dark wood. Fourteen miles south were his wife and daughter—it wasn't supposed to end this way on a day in November before his mother came, not on the eve of their first Thanksgiving in the big house. Hell with it, he wouldn't let it happen.

Back in Utah he'd taught a history workshop for the elderly and in that class was ancient Harriot Bean whose memory uncoiled like rich cloth with flashing bits of her life clinging to every strand. She'd been a twenty-year-old telephone operator in Kanab, Utah, on the morning of December 7, 1941, when the lines had gone crazy over Pearl Harbor. The USS Utah had been sunk with two of her classmates from Kanab High, Leopard ball players, good looking kids with their lives in front of them. That evening she'd accompanied friends to the outskirts of town where they'd fired pistols, rifles, the odd shotgun, just pointed the muzzles into the dark and fired at the dark matter beyond. The barrel mouths flamed with each shot, the repeats echoing off Nine Mile Canyon. The night of Pearl Harbor in South Utah, just before Christmas, 1941. The story'd touched Joe, the thought of all those kids in the December chill, out there on the outskirts of town near solstice, the town itself on the fringe of the still-wild West. The U.S. a country at war, soon to drop the bomb fueled by uranium mined not sixty miles away from there they stood that night. And there was young, pretty Harriot Bean, her towheaded lover fresh dead across the sea, firing *one, two, three* into a place she could not see but now knew.

For some reason Joey threw the Model 11 in the front seat, a water bottle and two cans of pork'n beans. Gravel crunched all down the line to Barton Road where Renee'd seen a pair of roadrunners their first week, where every last minute had this glow to it, and Lara'd fed the neighbor's white-face heifers sugar from the palm of her hand through strands of barbed wire. A Morrilton station came in loud and clear and some light flitted through the clouds, silver at the edges. Joey recalled the *60 Minutes* feature on Chernobyl—how they'd had to pipe in classical music, sent it screaming out of semi-truck sized speakers twenty-four hours a day so the apocalyptic silence of the vacant city wouldn't drive the remaining workers shithouse crazy. Where the bodies of first responders lay plastic wrapped in wooden coffins, which were then wrapped in plastic and lowered into zinc coffins, and those buried beneath endless truckloads of hot concrete. How the notes had echoed off the buildings and streets where for some reason a dead deer hung from a child's swing and slide, the breeze ruffling its fur in some far-off dream.

The blue book instructed him to drive to Hector, home of the Warlocks, to hit the road and DO NOT TAKE PETS. Joey whistled Moondog from the great room, loaded her and slammed the tailgate. He was to tear out the NOTIFIED page and attach it to his front door, and go. Past the Goodnos—there sat Dewitt Elliott on the front porch with a can of beer between his legs, same sneer he wore that first day when Joey moved his family into the Elliott's house, a chest freezer full to the gills with meat out under the August sun for spite, his little dog hopped atop it, growling. Let the son of a bitch burn.

Persons living in Zone L were to take HWY 7 to Dover, then HWY 27 to Hector, or HWY 164 to HWY 105, then Gumlog Road through the cutoff where the white horse stood, then HWY 27 to Hector. Go straight to Hector High. Principal Waylow would meet you with a bag including toilet paper and toothbrush and assign you a spot on the gym floor. There was a heated Mens and Womens with running water. Joey read the fine print of Renee's hand—*if you're reading this, Joey, I love you.*

Moondog moaned in back—he'd forgot her food sack, but brought both bowls and the biscuit box. For a long time him and Renee had been able to communicate without talking. At first, she'd flip him off behind his back and he'd feel it, that middle finger wavering when they'd fought over something silly like hair spray or how to pronounce *flutist*, or song lyrics she'd learned all wrong as a girl before she got a hearing aid. But lately, these last few years, of a sudden Joey'd think, we really should go to Florida for Christmas, and Renee'd say, "I've decided to go see mom and dad for the holidays." Or, after a spring rain lifted fire bans, the yard ape schoolkids lit tire fires on spring days when the redbud and jonquil perfumed the afternoon and everything should've been alright. Joey'd sit on the back porch, sip vodka tonics and invent awful acts of revenge, and Renee'd say, "It's the fathers of those kids ought to have their things cut off."

Only not today—nothing on the radar. At the four-way stop where he could head one way or the other, toward Hector or back to R'ville where his good wife and daughter were no doubt being whisked to Morrillton that very second—Morrillton, not far from the Stepwell Family Cemetery out on the Trails of Tears, Solgahatchia where his grandmother'd been married under a sweetgum tree on Isbel Creek. A semi blew by, a logger from Highway 7 with its headlights on high beam, rolling like a bat out of hell, so the back draft sucked the Pathfinder's nose toward R'ville—maw of the meltdown.

Toward R-ville, Joey sped.

As always, Billingsly's donkeys were loose at dead man's curve, where on the day he'd arrived Joey'd witnessed this beautiful woman with hair coiling to her hips, decked out in white chiffon with a ten foot-train and diamonds shining in both ears, her lipstick neon, casting a Devil's Toothpick into the stock pond with a full photography shoot going on, bright lights flashing through her gossamer veil. White-gloved to the elbow, she sent her plug thirty yards a pop. He'd taken it as a sign, Joey had, but what kind? Who could say? He didn't know what to make of the bride-to-be casting a spinning rod in her wedding dress for a photo shoot. Maybe it was the foreshadowing of this very moment, Joey Harvell on the end of his days, flooring it toward Solgahatchia for the wife and daughter he so loved?

He'd hardly ever made this drive save on the occasion of funeral processions, the long line of American cars with their headlights on, a trooper in the lead. Once, Sheriff Marlan Hawkins had led them on a Harley Davidson, and the last time for Jimmy, Joey's kid brother who'd been killed in a one-car crash driving home from Conway after midnight. Him and Renee had only just physically met. The runaway to DC had shaken Josephine, and it happened just after that. Three times he'd been driven here, and then Jimmy, which broke his heart, how endlessly messed up that Jimmy was here, that such could happen in this world. What'd happened to Jimmy had broken him down until Lara'd come along and love had lifted his heart.

Bunker Mountain to Wesley Chapel and the old gaunt Catholic church at St. Vincent to Wonderview, down the gravel road into Solgahatchia Bottom, Stepwell land, once. He passed hunt shacks and chicken houses to the lightning struck tree and finally the place itself with its rusted gate and bushhogged grass and big old shade oak. The summer before they'd buried Si, he'd visited this place with the old man at happy hour on a rain day. His grandfather'd had a highball on his spot at the foot of PaPa Stepwell, smoked a pipe then knocked it out on his daddy's stone. "Get in Joker. Let's get," he'd said and drove away.

Here now, alone.

The sun's come out against the backbone of clouds so there's a silver ridge to the south and east. Uphill, beyond the big Oak, Jimmy's stone shines, the blocks have held, not too many weeds. The summer he'd graduated UA, Renee'd driven him down from Fateville in the Cougar O.W.'d given him after he'd bought Josephine a brand-new Town Car with the insurance money. He'd met them with a wheelbarrow and tools borrowed from a Lonoke bricklayer who'd played ball with Jimmy, the championship team, 1993. For two spring-fine days he'd cut a footing around the grave plot then set blocks in a six-by-eight square. Joey'd mixed mud with five-gallon bucketsful of pond water hauled up from a pasture below, the barbed wire fence in-between covered with white blackberry bloom. Witchdoctors rode each other and a wrist-thick cottonmouth swirled under a tree root. A crow cawed, and the sound of his hand trowel *shringed* through the cemetery and into the woods when he cut mud to cinder blocks, knocked them plumb with the trowel butt. Stepwells had laid stone around their dead since the beginning of time, fathers whose sons lay at their feet, and at those feet, sons and daughters and wives, but as far as Joey can tell, he'd been first to do so for a brother dead young. How Jimmy's face shone, his true smile and letter jacket, and the finish work was good, the fine seams and bed of pea gravel.

He shouldn't be here.

What he needs is to find his people, this second, Renee and Lara, he'd pray for them if he still prayed, a long time now from that, those days when it was all real—the holy ghost fire. When Grandmother Dee'd take him to a full-gospel meeting and all hell'd break loose, churchfolk dancing the hurkey-jerk. Somebody'd yell *Gog rajeth in the East, Magog in the west. God damns this world to hell.* He'd felt in every cell of his body, and at night he'd pray real prayers for O.W. to get sober, for them to somehow get money for food, and maybe rent the three-bedroom brick across the street from Carla Jane, so he could see her through the second story window wriggling into short-shorts split up on the sides. All those Sunday mornings, stained light staining the front of her choir robe, how Joey'd read and memorized songs in the hymnals and his favorite books of the Bible, triple X-rated *Song of Solomon* with its perfumed breasts and heaving body parts. Then Revelations, how those washed in the blood would climb up out of their graves to the clouds while those left behind suffered unspeakable shit.

November chill, the shiver's up his backbone. Joey gripped the wheel. He'd forgot to hang the NOTIFIED sign on his door, and now the stones shone so they might be seen from the moons of Jupiter and beyond. Here, where it has ended for his blood people, one-legged Si, at the foot of PaPa Stepwell and his own mother, Ella Fryer, who'd stayed forever young. Over there's Uncle Leo, the cemetery's lone college graduate, he'd got big in tomatoes and married Naveen, Si's sister who'd once argued a man to death. Babies were buried under little lamb stones and somebody lay beneath a miniature cannon, the balls stacked in a V. Higher up the hill, Jimmy, six-feet tall and sawdust bronze, those sky-eyes and shining beard. Harvell pulled the e-brake so it cricked, got out of the truck just as a brace of sunshine poured through. The two-doored gate squalled when he swung it open, walked in to join his people. There was something he was supposed to do, some important thing. His life meant something now, that's how it seemed. This conviction poured through his blood and an honest cry rose joyfully from his throat. Around him, on the grassy acres where brown-eyed Susan bloomed on a day in May when you bury your brother, there was a stillness, a quiet. And through that quiet leapt a big-antlered whitetail, over the barbed wire inward and the sun caught its tines.

Joey had just one split-of-a-second to think *bright wings!* before his people commenced to claw themselves from their graves. In all directions, that's what happened, and he heard voices speak a language never heard, but known. Leo and Si and MaMa Stepwell joined the host he recognized by those features he and now his daughter shared.

They were on him, jubilant, dancing the holy ghost dance, a wreathed and shimmering array with hands thrown into the blue piece of sky where silver-rimmed clouds had just now ruptured, so the first of them treaded brisk air. They looked back with angelic faces, calling them by name, *come, come, come. Brothers, sisters, lovers in Christ. Look! We shall not perish.* How they beckoned him.

And then on the hilltop he witnessed his brother resurrected, how he stood to his full height, so different in face and body from the last time, the time carved into Joey's head. His white raiment shone, *radiant* and *radiant* and a thing beyond *radiant.* A horn blast blew from on high, and there was singing, and this was holy. The embrace lifted him skyward, where his maternal grandfather walked on two legs amongst the newly risen. Black folk, red and yellow and white, the fierce beauties of his childhood and the time before that, a whole troop of Cherokee with the gleam in their braids, arrayed and glimmering, the Eagle Chief on a skyward Appaloosa. The Trail of Tears would dry now. Joey watched himself drag the extension cord into the basement shadows, the muddy waterline's hiss and pop.

The image of wife and daughter gripped him.

How to turn face from this world, shed earth-skin and walk toward a home in glory that outshines the sun?

What the Newly Dead Don't Know but Learn

My cousin found a hand-grenade in a Camp Robinson stock pond that summer, pulled the pin and tossed it at me. *Die, fucker*, he said, and took off horseback in a cloud of Arkansas dust. The thing thudded at my feet where I froze, just shut my eyes and waited. That's how it was that summer, dry, no rain since springtime when Grandfather Harvell's Magnolias had bloomed like big white hands and Mama and Daddy had started burning each other's clothes in the backyard trash drum. I got sent to live with Uncle Earl, her crazy brother who ran Diamond T Stables, weekend trail rides for a $100 a pop on Camp Robinson, this vast commune where the Guard trained and it was not uncommon to find a booby-trap behind every bush. Somebody'd brought a dog that carried a live box turtle around in its mouth—the head and legs appearing then disappearing, *here-gone*, *here-gone*, the dog didn't seem to care two shits either way. Mama'd thought it a good idea for me to help Uncle Earl with his trail ride business, though what I mostly did was ride in the back of the pickup with Butchy, his derelict son, up to the car lot—Uncle Earl's *other* business—to pump up tires on all the jalopies that had gone flat overnight. For lunch we'd sit in the air-conditioned office that was cold enough to hang meat, eat cheeseburgers from the stand across the street, and Earl would drive out Asher to meet Maxie, his girlfriend. This one afternoon, three boys our age walked into the car lot office and tried to rob us, only Butch pulled Maggie out of its hideout holster under the desk, waved the .357 magnum in their faces, so they ran out the door into the heat screaming and we didn't see them again. The trail ride business—I don't know how all that started, but that's what everybody in Saline County with a hundred bucks wanted to do that summer, pack saddle bags with hot whiskey and ride. Maybe it was the weather that made everybody crazy. Twenty some had signed on, their horse trailers all parked in the base parking lot, tents spread across a field where wild daisies bloomed right up to the algae-covered pond where Butchy'd sliced open his heel on a broken bottle before finding the grenade.

I'd seen Maxie sneak into Earl's white teepee, followed by the spotted dog with the turtle wriggling in its mouth. Mike Smith—this friend of Earl's who was training to be an Oaklawn jockey though he was way too big—saw it to, and we both heard. Mike was currying the mane and tail of the Palomino he'd broken that summer, a spirited horse who neighed at the other horses with nostrils flared, whose eyes were curious and human-like—you could see the horse figure what was coming next—it was amazing. *May Day*, he was called.

Somebody'd said the dog thought he *owned* the turtle, that it was his possession, I remember willing it to live and out came its head. If you got close enough to see, some family or another had painted their names on the bottom of the shell, only it was from twelve years ago when I wasn't even born yet, the oddness of that. My Welsh pony was trained to lay down and hold his breath, a good trick because I could ride out ahead of everyone else and say, "Blaze, lay down and hold your breath." Up Maxie rode on her big paint. "*Oh!*" she cried out, the same word that she screamed inside Earl's white teepee. "*Oh!*" she said. "*He's bloating.*"

The paint stamped its feet, snorted. "Be still, goddamnit," she said, hooked a heel in the stirrup and swiveled off and wrapped both perfumed arms around me, so that I could smell her dark hair, like magnolias in a bowl at the center of the dinner table while mama prayed a too long prayer. "I'm sorry, son," she said.

I waited, breathing her in, that much I'd learned.

"Get up, Blaze," I said, and the horse straightened its front legs, hopped up and shook the dirt off, trotted to me, nuzzling my arm with a nicker.

"*You,*" Maxie said. She frowned. "Ever heard of the boy who cried wolf?"

I wouldn't say a word, because she'd tell Earl who was likely to beat you with a buggy whip, as I'd seen happen to Butch more than once.

I had no idea where the main trail ride was going, but I'd learned to let things roll out the way they rolled out. The hand-grenade lay at my feet. I was afraid to move, just like I had been when mama screamed out for me to get help, that O.W. was killing her. The sky was sky-blue above my head. There was a lot to think about. I mean, should you pick up a hand-grenade and throw it back? Run like hell? Go pull Maxie off Uncle and tell? Do nothing? As I ever had, I chose the latter and it brought us bad luck that very day.

Uncle had decided we'd swim the river that afternoon, cross the particular bend he'd chosen the week before when he'd driven out and camped overnight, probably with Maxie and her big paint. Horse people were funny—what class you were from kind of disappeared—shoveling shit was shoveling shit. This was Arkansas in July, and let me say two things about that. One: July is maybe not hot as August, but ungodly hot all the same—even the witchdoctors riding each other's backs seemed dazed, drunk with heat and there was zilch for breeze—the only relief, water. Two: when you're twelve, you haven't thought of some things yet, like the fine line between the truth and a lie, and that gap in-between that breathes in and out with a mystery all its own. You've sensed it, maybe even believe you can control it, but you haven't thought it out and understood the repercussions. What I'm saying is that, if you tell a lie, like your horse has lain down and died up the trail, then, when they ride up on it, yell at the thing to get up and it does. You see them shake their heads in disbelief, and it's possible that you could start to believe that you actually did have miraculous powers. I mean, you could start to believe your own bullshit about raising the dead. Well, it's possible, at least it was for me that summer. Who could blame me—my people were really fucked up—I had it in my blood by osmosis.

So Uncle Earl decided to swim horses across the Saline River on Camp Joseph T. Robinson Military, just like he'd seen in John Wayne westerns where a bunch of cowboys swam equines and cattle across some western river, which I've since learned is a crock, the west is dry, three rivers maybe, max. Despite the heat and drought, the trees were green that day, and the riparian shade was pleasing. Earl led us right up riverside on Chico—a thick-necked stud that was unstoppable once he took off, so Uncle'd replaced the chin strap with a strand of barbed-wire that bloodied the white whiskers. Butchy followed his daddy on Sugarfoot, a small gelding, but stocky and real spirited, a strong swimmer, right up to the water's edge, where Uncle climbed down out of the saddle, picked up a stick and sat cross-legged in the dirt.

"Swimming a horse is not complicated," he said, and drew a sweeping *S* into the dirt with the stick, marking the appointed spot in the river bend, where a low-swung tree had some moss hanging off. "Set your ferry angle against the current, lay out on his back and hang onto the saddle horn. Mike will follow me, then Maxie."

Maxie's paint nickered and May Day snorted—the stock knew something was up.

"We'll take out here," he said, marking an X lower in the bend. "Any questions?"

A cowboy wearing new shiny boots with gleaming spurs and a felt Stetson sipped from an army canteen and I saw Butch off to the side, poking a stick into a crawdad hole.

"What about life jackets?" the cowboy asked. "Don't we need life jackets?"

Uncle looked at me for some reason. He had a soft spot in his heart, because Mama was his only sister, and they'd been through the ringer growing up Stepwells, and now it was happening all over again to me. "Naw," Earl said. "Just hang onto your hoss. Okay?"

He swigged at his canteen, the fake cowboy.

The water was brown, chestnut color, the hue of Blaze's mane and tail, that's what I remember, that and how personal floatation devices seemed like great, good sense. This all happened in the days before release forms and such, so a good lawyer would lick his lips at a moment like this—people who'd paid money for a trail ride getting swum across an unfamiliar river on a military commune by a man who'd never thought to purchase insurance against accidental drownings or water poisoning or whatever such danger could be ferreted out of such a situation. Maxie wore a yellow bikini top, one of the straps falling off her shoulder. I'd seen a cottonmouth riding the current downstream. It wasn't swift or anything like that, just a wrist-thick snake slipping down the current mid-river, before all the grownups in our party rode over the marked S, passing from dirt into water, so the air was strong with fly dope and saddle leather, and the snakey smell of the mindless river itself, coiling through that summer afternoon that severed me from my childhood.

Earl swam first, big white Chico launching into the cool eddy, so you could see his forestocks glow, even through the murk, read the bloody mist beneath the open mouth. Then Mike Smith on May Day, Maxie on the paint, and a couple other adults in new cowboy hats and boots, the fear and thrill of what they did, how one feels, I'd later learn, when entering white water that has taken a life, the water has personality, you can feel it. Butch rode Sugarfoot. Blaze would do anything I asked, so we followed last—I was sweeper. A crow caw-cawed over the creek then, so its black-cross shadow fell across our path, and that's when it happened, mid-river, Uncle Earl screaming for us to turn back now, turn around and swim back. *Turn around*, he said. *Don't follow.* I'd just lay full out on Blaze's back, both his front hooves pawing water, thinking how uncannily cool this was, how easy and sweet to swim horseback. And neck reining a horse around in full swim is easier demanded than done, I've never seen it happen in any John Wayne western, not once. But Blaze obeyed and we climbed up the undercut bank, onto a table-rock that offered a full-view of the scene that still plays out before me on nights when the house gets quiet and I can hear my wife and daughter breathing.

My people are crazy. *Good-crazy*, Mama'd say, though I've never understood what evolutionary advantage there is to having such a predicament in your bloodline. Mama's daddy cut his own leg off with a chainsaw while on a firewood expedition up on Danville Mountain, then hemorrhaged all the way to St. Mary's where an emergency surgery saved him, but only by the skin of his teeth. At seventeen, Mama eloped with an Air Force man who claimed that his father was governor of Arizona, only it turned out his daddy was a dwarf and they lived in a screenless trailer next to a Tucson plasma center, which means my own children could be dwarves—my children's children. After I was born, she left him, but he followed her back to Arkansas and tried to kidnap me outright, only my grandmother somehow got him thrown into Tucker Prison Farm where he picked peas for one whole summer. Then mama married O.W., who'd been drafted as an outfielder for the New York Yankees, a flattop he-man that nobody fucked with, not even Uncle Earl, who was maybe craziest of all. Once, during spring run-off, Uncle Earl'd strapped one of those cheap-shit orange life jackets onto me and another on Butchy, threw us into Mulberry River—Arkansas's premier white water—for the sixteen-mile float through overhangs and strainers, amongst the most awful flotsam imaginable. We crawled out at the river bridge outside Opelo, half-drowned, caught a ride in whatever car lot jalopy he'd had driven out for the occasion, drove back and did it again—three times in all over the course of the weekend flood. Other times he'd have us jump off high things, cliffs and trees, a roof or two, and once he'd tied a Labrador Retriever to Butchy's foot, then slung them off a tree swing into Hurricane Creek. He wasn't right in the head, Uncle wasn't, but he owned a business, which made him respectable in Mama's eyes, enough so to keep me while her and O.W. killed each other. So it's no surprise what was about to happen, Mike Smith screaming *May Day, May Day,* the big Palomino neck-hooked on a fisherman's trotline, run straight down the middle of the S-bend in the river

Witch doctors rode each other over the flat rock to the bank where a king snake had shed blue skin. The rest of the trail riders were off their horses on the shore, some crying out and some just staring, the way you look at a house on fire. Butch had unslung his lariat, stood knee-deep in the current with it dangling. Out there were Uncle and Mike Smith, both swimming circles with Chico now, whose bloody chin shown in the watery glare. May Day's eyes, even from where I sat, flashed in their sockets and the neighing began, a pleading sound cadenced to the rhythmic churning of hooves. The horse pawed water in a frenzy of muscle so the whole trotline was visible, silver hooks gleaming at measured intervals to unseen tie-offs on the far banks. I'd set this sort of line myself, those summers down on Lake Ouachita, when I'd go out with Si, my mother's one-legged father, with a roll of hundred-weight nylon line and a sackful of treble hooks. Rocking in his flat-bottom, we'd tie one end to the trunk of an overhanging Cyprus, stretch line across the entirety of a deep water cove, then tie three-foot lengths of cord every six feet or so, and from these loop-knot fresh-sharpened hooks. Fish bream beds all afternoon until we'd scored a bucketful of bluegill, shoulder hook each and sink the whole thing with forty-pound rocks on either end. After midnight, we'd run the lines in the dark, careful, because Si'd known a man who'd drowned this way. "Hello? Are you listening?" the old man would say, then guide my hand to the quivering line, where it felt like we'd hooked a Volkswagen somewhere out there. Hand-by-hand he'd haul us toward what swirled in the dark. That was the kind of line May Day had swum into that afternoon in July when I was twelve, my mother and stepfather were trying to kill each other and I'd begun to believe that I possessed special powers.

Maybe five minutes passed and I don't think anyone knew what to do—it's like that, watching a drowning. People scream for you to help them, the beg and plead and cuss and pray, but finally there's not a whole lot that can be done, and you can't turn away even. Butch was crying, the lariat swinging at his knees. His daddy was out there in the water—and it dawned on me that he loved his old man as much as he hated him. May Day was full-fight now, *bleating*, so that the sound got inside of you and caught fire like listening to Jethro Tull's flute playing on acid. Black hooves with silver shoes made ruckus in the water, lifting the white line again and again so it showed its silver stringer of hooks for twenty feet in either direction, a nice channel cat on one down the line. Mike Smith and Uncle Earl, they clung to Chico who was fighting water too now, close enough for one of the hooks to catch any of the three. Earl was white-faced, his saddle bags spun in an eddy. I could see the resemblance between him and my mother, the widow's peak and earthy eyes, the countenance with which they both faced death, and that's when I thought of my knife. I remembered laying in bed listening to O.W. beat Mama, the sound of him slapping her down, and her all the time crying, "Get help, Jack, he's killing me." That's what she screamed to me—those exact words. And I'd just lay there, shivering, and he'd come to believe that I'd never lift a hand to stop him, and was so emboldened.

Cold water is heavier than warm, so there was a layer about four feet down that chilled my toes and then my foot, and then a hole where the current undercut the bank and I could feel the current, the power in the water. This as I slipped down, the unfolded Old Henry in my right hand. From this level, my eyes were even with the surface plane of the water and I could feel the horse screaming, a terrible sound to hear from there, a strong horse drowning. May Day'd disappear entirely, then fight his way up again, the screech constant now, the mush in his breathing, a plume of blood in the violent water. The line must be cut, I'd have to dive down, take it in my hand and saw with the other, then coax May Day to swim toward the other end, that's what I was thinking, dog-paddling at twelve, scared, my heart beating in my throat, picturing what must be done.

May Day was real, beautiful flesh and blood, tiring, about to give in to it all. Ten feet in front of me, the water swished in his lung. His eyes flashed, and we looked into each other's eyes there at the same level for a moment, long enough. I could read his mind and him mine in that second. *It's okay, son*, he was thinking, *it's all of us got to face our demons.* The knife escaped my hand. And there in front of me, close enough to touch, the horse sank beneath the brown water and was still.

For a long time and maybe by mistake, my mother tried to contact me from the grave. It would happen in the middle of the night, me asleep beside my good and patient wife, and the phone would ring out three or four times off-kilter. When I picked up (which is real hard to do when you're scared shitless) no one was there, not even a breath. Then I'd crawl back in bed and hear her call my name—just like that, say my name right through the walls. It was creepy. It scared the Jesus out of me, though you must know that we were close. With me never meeting my father, she was like my sister almost, and after she drowned, I delivered her elegy with true joy in my heart for her life, despite the evil Baptist preacher who wanted to turn the moment into a guilt-fest and rub everybody's face in it. But then I'd hear her voice in the night, over and over and over, it was no dream.

Buddhists believe the body goes on a forty-nine-day journey after death—they call it *bardo*, the time before the soul reaches the other side. But the soul has to be willing. If somebody's a victim of foul play, for instance, say they were drowned by somebody who was supposed to be delivering turkeys in goddamn Rocky Mount, North Carolina, someone who snuck up behind them and shoved their head under the water of their own hot tub, well that soul might not be cool with going on a *bardo*, they might be pissed off and have some talking to do. I don't know about all that, but I know for certain, without a glimmer of doubt, that Mama tried to talk to me from the grave, and it got so that I couldn't stand it, even though I missed her with my whole heart. Finally, in a way that unsettled my wife until her own mother died and she did the same, I yelled out in the dark. *Leave me alone*, I screamed. *Leave me the hell alone and die.* Around that time, her voice went away, and she has not spoken to me now for a long, long time.

Blaze swam up behind my back. I heard the soft nicker, turned, grabbed a hank of mane and let him swim me to the shore where Mike Smith lay on his face weeping, inconsolable for an hour or more there until the shade came on and the cicadas kicked in and he finally climbed up behind Uncle on Chico and was ridden back to camp. He wanted to be an Oaklawn jockey, but he'd gotten too big. May Day, the golden Palomino with knowing eyes, had been his solace—he loved the horse, and had finally had to retreat and let it drown. One of the fake cowboys had prayed out loud, then produced a pistol that looked like a toy compared to Maggie. Mike had thrown it in the water, where it lay loaded, probably, to this day. Back at camp, as dark came on and all those lightning bugs stung the bitterweed, Mike sat shaking his head. He set on a five-gallon bucket and shook his head.

It had fallen to me and Butch to unsaddle all the horses, feed and water and stow gear while an officer from Camp Robinson questioned Uncle Earl and some of the other adults. We loaded the horses into trailers, and it was dark-thirty when we rolled out. By the time we made it back to Diamond T Stables, it was after midnight. I was conked out in the truck seat beside Butch when Uncle backed the trailer to the front gate, loosed the horses in a side pasture. Blaze stood out there, staring at me in the rearview. He'd suffered himself to play dead at my bidding, then leap to life upon command. Could a horse fathom irony?

I allowed myself the vision of the three of us—me, Mama and O.W.—gone to see a movie on a February night. It was *Jungle Book*, and they held hands as big talking apes danced across the super-wide screen. We walked out and were hit in the face with an unpredicted snow, big flakes, silver dollars, our Pontiac covered already. "Ho, ho," O.W. sang out, skidding on his boot heels. Face to the sky, Mama seemed stunned. "Pixie dust," she said, and threw big handfuls up into the frosty air that was cleansed, that night, of the stench from paper mill further south.

Earl left us in the truck cab, walked into the house and a light came on in the kitchen. I'd once seen him shoot a dog with a bow and arrow right out the front door. It was a neighbor's dog, a barker, and he'd just pulled back and shot the thing, just like that. I imagined him inside at the kitchen table, thinking how he'd marked our passage into the dirt, how he would always be the man who'd scribed the perfect entry into the S-bend.

I was twelve that year and the world looks a whole lot different from this side. I have a child now, a girl who's twelve, big beautiful eyes like her mother and her mother's mother. She plays piano, and sometimes when I cook late in the afternoon, I weigh the notes falling and rising and falling like this shimmering waterfall. The horse and I had looked each other in the eye right there at the end. I'd swum out from the world of guilt and sorrow, with an unfolded knife and trembling heart. I'd been too late, sure, but I can live with that. Those afternoons while I mash garlic into the skillet, throw tomatoes and parsley into the sizzle, I listen to my daughter play the notes and wish Mama could hear this song, that she would forgive me and speak to me and not be dead.

She drove us to the family cemetery once, a road that paralleled the Trail of Tears, Choctaw land that the Cherokee had once been forced to walk, out past Lanty, Arkansas, into the Stepwell bottoms where every barbed wire fence was blown over with honeysuckle and blackberry. There, on a hillside that overlooked a lightning-struck tree, Stepwells were laid to rest at the feet of their fathers for the generations since they'd walked down from Henry County, Tennessee. We found our people's stones high on the hill, and I remember that black-eyed Susan was blooming. A rain had fallen and someone had turned loose dogs. Off in the hollow, we could hear them bay. Mama yanked weeds from the white pea gravel that covered her daddy, then lay a fistful of fresh picked flowers beneath his carved name.

"Looky here," she said, and stepped off to the old man's feet. "This is my spot. And you'll be there, Joe." She pointed, "Right beside me."

I looked at it.

Then Mama stood on her spot, and I on mine. She reached out a hand and I took it. She swayed one way and then the other and there, with no one watching, we danced, just shook ourselves on that piece of earth, the dogs howling in pursuit now, about to tree. The sun came out and the land below us seemed to shake itself off and be new. My mother laughed, her voice high and silvery like a girl's.

We fell down laughing, I don't know why.

A Funeral for the Living

Instead of a funeral, Captain Rockerson threw himself a week-long party that culminated in Miss Space Coast leaping *au naturale* from a sugar-glazed cake. The family was spread from the backyard pool deck through the rest of the house, and back to the Florida room, for it was an occasion that merited talk, wine, thirty dozen clams and a wheelbarrow full of fresh grouper that brother Rock, who Renee wasn't speaking to, had dived up from blue water with a spear gun. The Captain's cousin who was an expert on Newfoundland dogs had talked nonstop about the amount of oil on the skin and how bathing more than once a month was a no-no. He'd lost his wife the month before so he was already in full funeral mode. Lara and Ray and Angel were making their phones sing chipmunk songs and all the flat surfaces that weren't being eaten on were lined with albums stuffed with photographs from across the ages of Rockersons, many dating to the ancestral farmhouse in New Jersey that was now a museum of the last working farm in Plainfield. A sizzling day on the eleventh of June, the island house sits three blocks from the ocean on one side, and two blocks from the Indian River on the other, so there's the tang of salt water and oleander in the air, just like there'd been that distant June when mama'd drowned out of the blue in Arkansas while we were here celebrating Cap's 70th. Now, on the eve of his 84th, the old man holds forth from the dining table, surrounded by his brother Chuck's sons, 6'6" both of them with big Rockerson feet and wide country smiles, good blood in them, here from Vermont and Texas, with thirty some of the rest of us, summoned to Melbourne Beach for Cap's living funeral.

The new wife, Cap's, was once the island's hairdresser who herself had done Meg's red dye and permanent, is out back at the card table with Uncle Daryl, her Aussie diphthongs audible through the sliding glass doors. Brother Rock delivers yet another trayful of clams from the boathouse grill, spreads them table to table and into the house, sluicing butter melt and lemon juice on the Italian tile. I'm alone in the pool, a vodka tonic in a plastic glass with a wedge of good homegrown citrus, and it's odd, because I see the whole thing happening down to brother Rock's new blonde fiance's heel flouncing under the card table, Cap gesticulating through the glass at the big dining table where I've so often broken bread.

Uncle Daryl has just launched into the story of how a ninth-grade girl at the ritzy prep school he headmasters had been photographed performing oral sex on one of the senior boys down in Corpus over spring break. The photo'd somehow been forwarded to the entire student body and their parents, including the seventy-one mothers who showed up mad as hell on the Monday after break.

"Her father is a prosecutor. The girl who had her picture taken."

I'm in the water, up to my chin, it's warm, deep into happy hour, and I fight the urge to pee, then let go. Rock and Meg had moved down here twenty-three years ago, the same year Renee and I lit out for Utah and the wild west. The kidney-shaped pool has turtle mosaics winged on the floor, and some of the tiles have come unglued. Banana trees sprout just out of reach, and I remember how Uncle Chuck'd bought Lara a ten-foot plastic alligator to float on the week Mama drowned, how odd and out of place it had seemed after.

"So the photograph, this picture, goes viral and somebody calls me, says 'have you seen it?'"

"I said, 'seen what?'"

"It was the school attorney, a friend of mine, and she sent on straight away, but what do you do? I mean, it was spring break. The kids were down at Corpus. What am I supposed to do?"

Lara learned to swim in this pool. MeeMaw used to sit with her on the steps and get mad when Lara splashed her hairdo, and we'd all be lit up and there'd be ribeyes on the grill, jumbo shrimp on ice in the sink, those still afternoons within earshot of the Atlantic, sunburned, and it felt good to have a family, the food, liquor and wine, and funny-smart people like the Rockersons and Renee and brother Rocky, even, though his first wife Bet was an off-the-charts bitch, had actually argued a man to death once.

"So seventy-one mothers, *seventy goddamn one*, they were waiting in a line at the front door come Monday morning after break. The one they'd chosen as leader had an eight-by-twelve of the offending photo which she shook in my face. "What do you intend to do about this?'"

"I said, '*what?*'"

I'd waded to the side of pool nearest the card table where Daryl's audience was rapt, hung on every word, and it was a good story, he had my attention.

"And these women, they went ballistic, they said they'd have my ass, that the girl's father was the prosecuting attorney for Harris County, the fourth largest county seat in the goddamn nation, that the girl was drunk. She was sixteen. *Sixteen.*"

"So I said, 'ladies, you're right. She's too young to drink beer in Texas. But it was not on school property. You expect me to police spring break?"

At this, the woman who was leader had sneered. Daryl sneered, and Annie laughed out loud, Rock's new fiancé. "'*Drink?*' the woman said. 'Just which way does your moral compass point,'" she demanded, shook the photo in his face.

"As a matter of fact," Daryl said, "it's a US felony to transport porn across county lines, Ms. Dominquez, which is exactly what you've done by bringing this photograph with you today."

With this, he'd walked into the school where he was headmaster, a mansion on forty acres outside of town part of the deal, a 32' offshore fishing rig and RV in the drive—

all part of the package. "And I quit," he said. "Over a spring break blow job."

Brother Rock walked up that second with another tray of clams. "Here, here," he said, "sounds like fun." He grinned at Annie and dumped shells from one side of the table to the other, everyone launching into their own stories on a related theme, and on it went into the night on the eve of the Living Funeral, a white pavilion tent and fifty chairs set up this side of the boathouse, the sky going pink now, pink sky at night, sailor's delight.

Captain Rockerson walked out the sliding glass door, Rose at his side. Everyone's in shorts and sandals, sated with food and wine, and a little unsure about what exactly you do at such an event. Out comes Renee, my good wife, behind her father, then Lara, Ray and Angel. Every one of us is outside under the sky with the waving palms swishing and the kind dark coming on, the air sweetened by the odors of a thousand blooming things, the ancient loggerheads heaving out of the surf up to the dunes to lay eggs in dark places.

"Here, here," Cap says. "Thank you all for coming. Our ceremony is tomorrow at 1:30. Casual. A catered dinner will follow." Here the old man choked up ever so slightly. "There's Bailey's inside for anyone who wants it."

"Here, here," Daryl said. "Thank you," Uncle Rock," he said, stood and applauded. I climbed out of the pool, dripping. And we all stood there and applauded the moment, clapped for the great good idea of coming together in a happy time, and whatever it would come to mean to have done so.

Overnight, there's a mass shooting in Orlando. We couldn't know that, of course, though our night at Sandy Shoes, a mom-and-pop hotel on the beach side, did not pass entirely in peace. Friday night, the place was jammed, nearly thirty kids in one room, I'd learn, and they all went apeshit in the center courtyard pool all our rooms faced, the second-floor balcony just right for a head-splitting leap into the deep end which these wild awake teens, stoked on who knows what, were going at just after midnight when we called the police the first time. Renee made the call, she was pissed, had yelled alternately BE QUIET and SHUT UP out our second story door to gleeful laughter. The cops came, and everyone seemed to go to bed, and then there was a pounding on our door whose bolt lock was broken, so the thing came opened a little, and whoever was out there pounded some more.

Lara never budged.

Renee got up to pee.

I unfolded a six-inch Buck knife and retrieved the biscuit rolling pin from the kitchen with its one window overlooking the beach north toward Cape Kennedy, stood just inside the slammed shut door afraid to look out, sure to God one of the kids we'd called the cops on had staked out our room, had a rifle scope on unit 8's front door, the dinky lock opened with the code 8727 which I remembered because I was 27 in '87. Another pounding came on the second door, just outside Lara's bed in our bedroom, and through the shut blind I caught a flash of metal, and that's when I opened the door and stepped out, the rolling pin held high. Renee was behind me. I could hear her breathe.

Because of the turtles, lights were banned, so we stepped like that into the most beautiful Florida night, on the second-floor catwalk above the pool, the bright stars reflected in the Atlantic to my left and twinkling beneath the clear chlorinated water, dark shapes moving in the surf, sister turtle swum into the dark place to dig holes in the dune with flippers, lay eggs and swim back to kingdom come. We breathed sweet air. No one was there. A phantom had beat on both our doors. Out near the dumpster and the street, the neon Sandy Shoes sign flashed on the highway, lit it up just enough to see it was there, connected to the Eau Gallie causeway and the way to Orlando where unspeakable shit was going down that second, fifty dead, that many again wounded.

"Coast clear?"

I said, "I think so."

She laughed, Renee, a sailor's daughter, she'd grown up near the sea and it always did something for her mood, made her different, good medicine. "I was afraid you'd roll somebody to death, dough boy. Look, there's the dipper."

I could smell her skin, the saltwater in her hair.

"And I don't think I've ever seen a man in tighty-whities with his rolling pin out on the beach at night."

Across the way, a blind fluttered. The tide was coming in, riding the pull of a full flower moon.

From the front door of our hotel to the ocean was a minute's walk, and it's my habit to go there straightaway, the big orange ball of sun rising from the green water, the heat not so brutal now, and the water, once you're up to your neck at about a hundred yards, a carnal delight. Some kids from the bevy of wild women who'd rented half the place were finding sand dollars with their feet, a slew of them at that exact depth and distance from the beach, diving for the living crustaceans then letting them submerge again. Two of the wild blondes who form a beach circle each night and drink themselves silly while singing James Taylor paddle out on standup boards, leap to their feet once past the last breaker, and stroke paddles in the pond-slick water heading south. An osprey sails overhead, snagged whiting wriggling in its claws. There are no clouds this early. A dozen sets of turtle tracks, some three feet wide, mark the quarter mile of beach up to Sandy Shoes. After Meg died, we came here to this space, walked the beach to an isolated stretch, sat cross-legged in a mama turtle's tracks and burned sage. She'd decided at the last minute not to go home for her mother's last birthday, and that was hard on her, it still is.

Brother Rock had absconded with the painting Renee'd framed for her mother because it reminded her of Phillipi, West Virginia where Meg had grown up, Andrew Wyeth's *Christina's World*, which turned out to be a study of his neighbor who was crippled by polio. Renee'd walked right into her brother's master bedroom, took the painting down and shipped it to Salt Lake, just like that. It's a hard time, when your people die, and you need to hold a piece of them to your heart, when the sad organ music washes over you in church and the weeping is from way down deep, a hurt that heals and goes on hurting.

Just as I think it, the saltwater sluicing over me, there she is, Renee, her big Rockerson physique, the sun in her eyes, she wades through a hip-deep breaker and takes three hard strokes toward me, the paddle boarders out of sight now, their children tired of sand dollars. Down the beach an old man is running the beach access stairs at Ponce de Leon Landing. Shirtless, his grey hair shines.

"The little bastards dug up eggs. They messed up the whole dune." Her foot touches mine, and it's good being in the ocean with her so near sunrise. "They threw them out. The manager did this morning."

I said, "Good morning."

"There's watermelon cut in the fridge. I made coffee." She lays back, floats, brown-skinned already this early in summer. Her hair's lightened. Who'd of guessed we'd make it to double nickels, 55, me and Renee?

"Someone was knocking. Remember?"

She splashes the good chill water in her face. "The desk woman came up. She said it was our neighbor. The lady forgot her code and what room she lived in. What she gets for singing Sweet Baby James all night at the top of her throat."

Walkers on the beach, they head north and south, barefoot, some with shoes, young and old and in between, always a hot one in a string bikini, full aware of the whole world's gaze, the odd one with a metal detector seeking Spanish gold, runners and jumpers and shell seekers, everybody looking for something.

"Dad said a ton of tequila washed up. Just after we left Christmas. One of the cargo crates tumbled. They can't tie them. The ship would flip in the wind."

We're walking against a rip, not bad, but a good pull south to north, walking out the riptide but not moving.

"Do you think we'll come back when he's gone?"

I said, "There's Rose. Rock and Ray and Angel."

"I dread this."

I said, "Is Lara still asleep?"

"Don't drink too much."

The paddle board blondes zip the current in our direction—our age, maybe younger—pass us by and keep on going. Way off on the Sandy Shoes access, a figure one would discern at this distance as an athlete, rugby, maybe, tall as me and muscled, Lara holds a hand to her brow and smiles, I see her smile from two hundred yards. She waves. Renee and I wave back. The water is cool and sweet.

"Let's go eat," Renee said. "I'm going early to set up."

"I love you."

She touched my face, nodded, then squealed. "*Fish,*" she yelled and took off swimming. Sure enough, a school of baitfish was on us, something big cutting through, so swerves of green and silver fin flashed this way and that, and it was best to get one's body the hell on out of the water.

Everyone on the island knew every last thing about everybody else, and none so much as Rose, the captain's new wife and island hairdresser, who asked us, when we walked through the big wood door into the house where the funeral for the living was moments from beginning, "Have you been watching the news?"

Lara carried a bag of ice in each hand, dripping already. She'd worn a summer dress and leather sandals, was beautiful, a woman now, on her way to the university and the rest of her life.

I said, "No ma'm."

"You haven't looked at your tv?" Out back the caterers from Charlie and Jake's Barbecue were unloading huge tinfoil trays of pulled pork and chicken, all of the sides. The steel drum player was setting up his steel drum. It was sunny and bright, hot as a firecracker.

I said, "What's up?"

They'd cranked the air down and Cap was nowhere to be seen. The cousin whose Newfoundland dogs served as airport distress agents every other week in upstate New York, he walked out the sliding door and under the big white circus tent, where seven big round tables were lined with chairs, flower arrangements and the condiments courtesy of Charlie and Jake.

"There was a shooting. An alligator ate the baby."

I'm not making this up.

Renee walked in that second, took the two ice bags from Lara, said, "We need help out here. The silver's not set."

"An alligator ate the baby?"

Disney World, an accident, the whole world looking at it.

From there on the day unfolded, on the heels of a sleepless night when pandemonium some miles away was distant as a moon landing, when the ancient monsters of our dreams had crawled out from the ornamental cement ponds of our making and snatched our offspring between cold jaws, when all manner of thing seemed any second not to hold, so commenced the living funeral of Captain Rocky C. Rockerson.

The foil was removed from the trays. A buffet line started. The steel drum player lit into *caribe* and we broke bread on a Saturday afternoon near the ocean.

Who was the man and why had he called us to him now? Who would have the gall?

This was 2016, Rock was turning 84, which meant he was born in 1932, the year the Dow Jones bottomed out at its lowest point of the Great Depression. It was Leap Year, the Olympics were in both Lake Placid and Los Angeles, and Babe Ruth made the home run call in Game 3 of the World Series. Folk listening to the radio heard Buck Rogers debut, the first of the star men imagined who'd walk on the moon thirty-some years later. The great war to end all wars was over and the century was young still and the millennium afforded space and hope. The nuclear nor the H bomb had yet to detonate, nor the rockets that would blast us to our sister planets and beyond. Humankind had only been capable of flight for a scant few years and had only barely begun to grasp the implications of Einstein's relativity, how it warped space and time.

Back in Salt Lake, Renee, Lara and I had witnessed the sort of funeral the military throws for a man such as Rock, the folding of the flag alone enough to floor you. Rock Rockerson was a good man. His wife had loved him, his children.

"Here, here," Rock said, stood to his full height at the head table. There was the ringing of a fork on a wine glass, and then silence. He turned to face us, Rose beside him, the steel drum gleaming and lush oleander growing up the fence. The linen had been pressed, *fleur de lis* folded into the wine glasses.

"I think everyone knows why we're here today. If not," he said, and his breath caught, "I'll say a few words about that."

Cancer, heart attack, stroke—they'd all had at him. Once, when we'd bought a farm in Arkansas, I'd pulled one fork of a tree off on his head with a pickup truck—Renee saw it happen from the back deck.

"A lot of times, when loved ones pass, we get thrown together in ways that are not good, are not pleasant or happy. Like I said, we have to drop everything and make emergency flight reservations at ridiculous rates. Then we get where we're going and whoever we're there to honor doesn't even know we're there. So I thought, why not bring our family together in a happy circumstance? Why not eat, drink and be merry together in a good way? That's what we're here for, why we've gathered."

In his hand, a gavel of all things.

"So when something happens to me, lift a glass of wine, think on this day, and don't wonder what they'll do with me."

He swung the gavel so it smacked the table three times. "And don't forget about Rose."

I imagined Meg here, Mama, Jimmy, Grandpa Si, Mom Dee and MaMa, Danny Turner, Mike Walton, Ron Neerling and Liz—the whole slew who'd passed over and all we could do for them now was tend their graves, talk to the stones, get heat stroke laying the Stepwell blocks around their sorry plights. All those who'd sailed off to sea and never come back, the bombed and brutalized through the ages, the Vietnamese and the soldiers whose names were chiseled on the black shiny stone, all the Trayvon Martins. The school kids and teachers at all of the Sandy Hooks that had ever been or will ever be, the marriage parties droned to kingdom come this day or that, the innocent dead in Orlando. I'd accompanied my grandfather on Mama's side to our family cemetery on the Trail of Tears near Solgahatchia Bottom north of Morrilton, Arkansas, and he'd had a drink of bourbon on his spot, smoked a pipe, showed me where Mama and Daddy and I'd be. He'd peed on his spot, right out under the blue sky, shook old charlie out and let fly.

There was a spattering of applause—just a little, who knew what to do? Finally, Uncle Daryl, 6'6" in loafers, stood amidst us, lifted a bottle of Corona, said "Here's to Uncle Rock. *Cheers.*"

"Here's to Rock," we all said. *Cheers.*

Then there was much cheering and laughter, hugging on the green lawn under the white circus tent. Cousin Sherry got thrown into the pool and brother Rock did a backflip in Bermuda shorts. The steel drum man sang Jimmy Buffett and the Newfy Dog cousin danced with Rocky's young fiancé, her blonde hair twisted into a french braid. We grazed through seconds and thirds of pulled pork sandwiches, short ribs and potato salad, barbecue chicken washed down with ice cold beer, and Dar, the clam woman dropped in with another bag of clams. A gigantic birthday cake came flying out, the numbers 8 and 4 blazing and the steel drummer led us in a caribe version of happy birthday which Lara sang in Spanish.

Out burst Miss Space Coast—Uncle D's idea. She was shy, washed off in the pool and kissed Cap on the cheek before leaving. Ray and Angel danced a boogeloo, and someone asked Rock to do the hokey pokey—which he did, big old man in khaki shorts, *you put your right foot in you put your right foot out*, and oh good lord did he ever shake it all about.

Finally, Rock passed the Rockerson gavel onto cousin Chuck, the patriarch of the clan now, and there were words, though mostly a joyful revelry in the moment that would soon pass, so we'd disperse, go find our beds and sleep within earshot of the ocean before flying home to the lives that remained before us.

The foil trays were recovered, and the ice melted in the coolers where beer and watermelon bobbed, and some of the funeral-goers went inside, their faces white with false light as evening came on, and the rest of us lounged full-bellied poolside. The steel drummer packed and left, a sheet of music wafting in the oleander. Ms. Space Coast had forgotten one of her heels, pink, the stiletto pump black and shiny so the hired man who took the tent down could see his face in it. Renee came to me and she smiled and said I love you, and I'm not sure how it all ended or if it ever did, Rock's funeral.

Arrangements had been made for the family to attend Sunday service at St. Sebastian's by the Sea Episcopal, where the altar flowers were given to the glory of God by Rock Rockerson in thanksgiving for a wonderful life, and the sanctuary candle signifying the presence of Jesus Christ in the Blessed Sacrament was given in the memory of Rock Rockerson's parents. Renee, Lara and I were five minutes late. We walked in during the reading of scripture—*Keep, O Lord, your household the Church in your steadfast faith and love.*

The air-conditioned air and smell of flowers.

All baptized Christians are invited to take holy communion, Renee falls back with her father, Lara walks with me. We go to our knees, open mouths, accept the host. Before us, and behind, there is family. Lara knelt beside me, behind me my wife, her father, my mother, my people, all of us, the cross and the stained light, outside the ocean rolling and heaving, the fat bulge where the full flower moon held its course for another day.

That we might love more fully, the father prayed.

We stood, that bitter taste in our mouths. Passed back through those who were passing forward, the big double doors soon to be thrown wide open so our faces would be bathed in light. We'd walk into the timeless ocean and the salt of its water would buoy our weight.

And one last thing.

A family photograph was taken after the backyard service—the steel drummer turned photographer, his shadow thrown behind us by the westering sun. There was the new patriarch of the Rockerson clan, gavel in hand. Order in the court. Order in the goddamn court. Our Lara, Renee, me, arm in arm. Azalea blooms violently behind us. The Space Coast, Gemini and Apollo and all those shuttles—blast offs to the Moon and Space Station, Mars, even, Jupiter, probing the edge of the Milky Way and beyond.

All here in the funeral for the living.

Swimmer

Cape Blanco. Oregon Coast. Summer 2015.

The fishermen wanted to be rescued.

They'd had enough. Thirty-knot wind in their faces and a fog ceiling, the sort of dark and head-high breakers that made them puke aft and stern in the life raft moored to the wreckage. The godawful rocks had chewed a hole through *Jamie K.* big as a Volkswagen, big enough to admit the monster head and jaws of the great white that had stalked them south. The engine room flooded. They'd lost power. Her *Mayday* had gone out lifetimes ago. Ten-thousand pounds of shrimp rotted in her hole, and leaked diesel slicked the Cape. Her skull-crushing outriggers whizzed over their bare heads. The unceded mast threatened. If they didn't untie, the son of a bitch wave would pitchpole them and they'd drown. The helicopter couldn't have arrived a moment sooner.

Swimmer saw this, and his heart was moved for the shrimpers. Those four—they were up shit creek.

The Coast Guard had flown an MH 65 Dolphin rescue helicopter from Group Air Station North Bend sixty miles north. Sheer winds nearly took them down twice before they ever made Blanco, the westernmost point in Oregon. There, an ancient lighthouse flashed every nineteen seconds to warn of the forty-nine documented perils of the head. On board: two pilots, a flight tech, and a swimmer named Harold Dare from Jupiter, Florida, who dropped on a hoist to the flare where four men in survival suits were going hypothermic.   Swimmer's first night rescue: he tasted diesel, salt, his own bile.

"Glad to see you," the white-faced one Dare took for captain said. Then the wench broke and the chopper blew into the cliff wall.

We returned to the chalky-white bluffs of Blanco, I guess, to seek the peace we'd found there after Mama died, that out of the blue drowning that coincided with Cap's 70th down in Florida, so we'd had to steal our rental Pathfinder and drive from a birthday party to a funeral. It would forever be crossed in my mind, how we'd driven home to Mama's birthday funeral, where I delivered a birthday elegy and watched them lower her into the birthday dirt of Solgahatchia on ancestral Stepwell land near Morrilton, Arkansas—cut through by the Trail of Tears. After, we headed West, drove clear to Oregon, as far away from the Natural State as you can get without swimming, and finally I did that too. Jumped my ass in the breakers and stroked out past Needle Rock where a grey whale and calf swam within a rock's throw of the beach for three days running, and where now the *Jamie K* was flipped on her side, rocking in the breakers, the black and white hull stark against the green water.

I studied her from the muddy camp, fitted out for handicapped campers, a concrete walkway for wheelchairs, steel railing, the site number raised in braille. It had rained.

The drive in had been a jolt.

Cape Blanco State Park—or at least the land on either side of its seven-mile entrance from 101 South past cranberry bogs and farmland—had recently been the site of a gargantuan hillbilly hootenanny, some 30,000 country and western fans with their RVs for the three-day concert that had coincided with the shipwreck. It had been difficult, we'd learn, to get the EMTs and ambulance in from Bandon. A crew of four fishermen had suffered terribly there. After the rescue copter's wench failed, they'd had to be swum one-at-a-time through seven-foot breakers, two hundred fifty yards from lifeboat to shore. A Great White had been sighted. Now, a thousand Honey Bucket outhouses stank to high heaven, blue blue windows as far as the eye could see.

The place felt invaded. A Confederate flag flapped on a silver pole, the hardware clinking. Renee's Subaru slowed. She rolled a window down and pointed. "Get a load of this," she yelled.

We made the camp loop three times. Our spot was taken, the RV big as a semi, with an awning stretched out over the place where we once lay with a light rain tapping our fly. The handicapped site on the lee side was open but muddy, a pine needle covered trail leading down to a fence where I caught site of the cape. There was the holy rock where we'd laced wildflowers into the mane of a bloated sea lion. Just north, something I didn't remember—the odd black and white trawler, on its side, low tide now, the rocks out there like sawteeth. We settled for campsite twenty-one, away from the bluffs overlooking the surf, protected from the wind and not two hundred yards from last time, when we forgot the days of the week and the mother whale and calf had swum just beyond the first wave, close enough to see her eyes, to be sure that she was looking at us.

She set the tent, our third since 2002, while I rigged the kitchen and lantern, laid out makings for happy hour: vodka, sliced lime, tonic. A Gatorade for Lara. Olives. The rest of the crackers.

It had rained last time.

Yellow bells bloomed.

Butterflies had flown over the campground and the sun came out and lit up their wings on a day with no name.

Lara was biking circles around Cape Blanco—the head jutting into the blue-cold ocean, building size rocks reefing far out into the sea, the stray ship glinting, the graveyard of the Pacific, it was called. She's grown now, so like Mama in the face. At seventeen, she'd forgot the song she'd sung for me when I hurt worst—*three elephants went out to play, on a spider's web one day*. She didn't remember the bouquet of wildflowers, how the rabbits had shied to the brush at camp's edge when we fed the pages of our calendar to a fire not unlike the one I'd kindle tonight, the chill on us, sun falling behind the holy face of cliff.

A sunk ship rocked on the rising tide, a Great White out there tagged with a radio receiver, patrolling the surf.

Swimmer had a story.

On a day when he was fourteen and I was forty, the young Dare surfed the break at Ponce de Leon Inlet, on the east Florida Coast below Canaveral, while five miles down the road I stood knee-deep in a blue run. This was July 14, 2002, the day Mama lay in an Arkansas hot tub, drowning. Swimmer—he was of course not called that then—had just kicked his six-foot board through a pod of baitfish gone crazy when a shark, a big bull, hit the board and bit off a piece of his hand. He didn't know this until he got to shore and saw blood dripping on the white board at his feet. The Global Shark Accident File for 2002 featured his youthful photo, the injured hand, and a report:

> Harold Dare, a fourteen-year-old male, was 5'10 and weighed 125 pounds. He was wearing grey board shorts, a black rash guard, and a black leash attached to his ankle. The surfer was using a six-foot Al Merrick white tri-fin board. The three fins were red. The sky was sunny and the air temperature was about 90 F. Waning Crescent moon, 1% of the moon's visible disk illuminated. The water was brownish, murky and underwater visibility was poor. The sea was choppy. People were fishing off the jetty. There were baitfish in the water and the surfer observed them jumping. The shark came from his right, struck his right arm and knocked him from the board. He walked/swam back to the beach. Dare's right hand was lacerated. The Beach Patrol cleaned the wound, and his mother drove him to Bert Fish Hospital. He arrived twenty minutes after the incident. The wound was cleansed and dressed.

Florida Today ran the story under the headline "Sun, Surf—And Sharks," only the bull had hit Swimmer like a freight train and he dashed out of the water so quickly that he didn't know what hit him until he saw the shredded hand. Experts claimed the culprits to be young fast-moving feeders that charge into a school of finger mullet as a moving smorgasbord, the blacktip migration following anchovies and pinfish south, stalking the inlets. Dare was back on his board the following weekend. He never missed a beat. "I try not to think about it," the teenage swimmer said, "I put it out of my head."

Swimmer showed the scar to a girl in the back seat of a jet-black Camaro parked in a gravel pit under the big swirling Milky Way in November, when the heat let off in Brevard County and the snowbirds had started to arrive from up East. A Peter Frampton cassette had just switched to side two, " Lines on My Face." The waves were breaking magnificently all down the Space Coast, the front end of Hurricane Kyle. She'd held the hand up so starlight shone on it through the tinted back window, the blue veins on the backside, the smooth groove below his thumb where flesh was missing.

"Shark medicine," she'd whispered, the chill *S* swishing through her teeth. She laced fingers through his, her thumb through the groove. "Yours fits mine."

Site twenty-one was at the mouth of a shaded opening where a house-girthed tree had taken the sky and in its fifty-foot circle of shade, a pair of pinyon jays had scavenged a package of Fritos about which they were raising holy hell. I threw a rock and the big birds flapped up a limb heckling, so Lara made a face, buried her head inside the bag. Renee opened her eyes, closed them. Out under the blue sky I fried bacon and eggs, made sandwiches and rolled blankets, tied them into day packs. We ate then, filled water bottles and a Ziplock of cashews, sports bars and extra sunscreen, my Buck knife and a blue tarp, what was needed to reenact that distant day when I'd made peace with my mother's drowning. There was the sound of the sea, just barely, and the jays were just too much, they flapped above us, caw-cawing, shitting on the tent from the highest limb. One of them distracted our dog, while the other dive-bombed the food bowl. This time my thrown rock skittered over the pavement to the next camp where a blank-faced Texan stared.

Tuesday, August 4, 2015, year of the wood goat. The Japanese had fired on this very spot, we'd learn. During World War II a submarine had started a fire with a water-to-air missile. Indians considered the place holy, would convene on the upper reaches for ceremony in the good stiff spirit wind. Whales had navigated the head forever, spouting their shimmering breaths.

They'd come for me last time. 2002, when I'd run into the surf just beyond the needle rock, swam hard away from the thought of Mama in a casket, under the wet earth of the Solgahatchia Bottom. I beat the water with his fists, right there where the shrimper'd sunk, where the rescue had taken place. Where Renee had built a makeshift shelter of driftwood, tied the blue tarp and formed a crude doorway, through which I eventually climbed, embraced her and Lara in the small light and took shelter from hard wind and was healed.

The helicopter hoist malfunctioned. In forty knot winds and pitch black, the rescue team had spotted the Jamie K's flare and dropped Swimmer in a basket and shoulder harness down where the four fishermen had taken to their lifeboat. Because of the wind, the Dolphin hit shear and had to do the drop from a hundred feet instead of thirty. Backflow had flown over the shield glass and all had got dicey. The pilot said, uh huh, not going to happen, and the useless hoist was retrieved by hand.

Four scared men waited in full survival gear, three thousand gallons of diesel slicking the breakers, fifty-six-degree water and the godawful wind, only outdone by the dark, a two-way riptide over razor-edged rocks, two-hundred fifty yards in, two fifty out—a swimmer would cover a mile in the water that way.

He'd of course trained.

And in that training was another story he'd not forgotten though he could not remember, for the life of him, the most important part, how his heart had stopped beating in an underwater lap, the subsequent rescue and resuscitation, the five days and nights in coma, waking to the faces of strangers, himself the most alien of all. He did not know who he was, Swimmer. He had not one shred of memory, not of himself or where he'd come from, what food he liked, or that a fish in the ocean once mistook him for food.

The man who saved Swimmer had come across him floating on the bottom of a lane, on his back with his face up and eyes wide open, staring up through the chlorinated water at the blue Florida sky.

Total amnesia, the specialists said, *tabula rasa*, Swimmer was a blank slate.

The gate that led from the overlook down to the beach was locked. NO ADMITTANCE, a hastily painted sign said. SALVAGE OPERATION IN PROGRESS. We stood there before the clearing where the world opened to the sea and fell down the steeply broken cut to the strand of beach scattered with driftwood from ancient conifers that lived in the day of Julius Caesar, if the brochure was to be trusted. DO NOT ENTER, a second sign said in a child's scrawl, NO ACCESS. A semi-trailer was parked outside the gate, loaded with spools of heavy cable, pipe and welding gear, a coil of clear oxygen hose and an iron platform. A Honey Bucket outhouse, the same blue as its thousand sister outhouses back on the road in, sat on board, with a plastic wrapped bale of toilet paper. Far below, testament to the truth of the locked gate, an engine sputtered.

"Vehicles," Renee said. A blue Indian blanket stood two feet out of her day pack and the canopy above her brought out the green in her hazel eyes. She'd saved my life that first year after—what love is, a buoy thrown when you're drowning. "They meant to say 'no admittance to vehicles.'"

Lara'd dreaded the hike—a day on a vacant beach with a whole lot of walking in heavy packs held no allure for her seventeen-year-old heart. That one time, before I swam past the needle rock, she'd walked a heart into the sand, heel to toe, her arms thrown out for balance, and then she'd looked up at me, smiled, and in her I saw Mama, only grown young again. "No, Mom. It means us. Dad, me and you. We can't enter."

Yesterday, we'd driven to the overlook road that led down to the lighthouse and seen the tiny divers in black wetsuits disappearing then appearing from under the Jamie K. There'd been no sputtering machines, nothing like that. A visible trail wound down from the parking lot to where they wanted to be. That's how they'd go. Down the cliff trail.

"We'll walk to the lighthouse and take the tour. They can't keep us out."

"Bull," Lara said.

A bulldozer followed by another bulldozer turned the corner—Caterpillars, Cats they're called.

"No admittance," Renee said. "What could that mean?"

"We can't go in, Mom."

"Well it's a mistake. It's an old sign."

The bulldozer man stepped from his machine, left it running so you could smell the diesel, feel the ground throb. When they'd built the trolley line in front of our house, many bulldozers and backhoes and jackhammers shook the ground until our house cracked right down the middle. The man tipped his cap, unlocked the padlocked gate, waved his mate through. He followed and the mate relocked the swinging gate behind them. The Cats rumbled down the road to our strand of ocean.

Renee said. "Damn."

"I've always wanted to drive one of those," I said.

The diesel turned my stomach.

Beside Lara the dog huffed and puffed, ready to go. We'd driven across Idaho, passed up over Blue Mountain toward Pendleton where the world opened and, like every other emigrant, saw what lay a hundred miles in every direction. The great Columbia Gorge hauled us through its corridor, and the energy of that ancient riverbed had carried us through Portland to where Highway 6 plunged down along the Wilson through old growth conifers to Tillamook where we had a first view of the sea. Bay City and Garibaldi to Rockaway Beach. I knew that it would all come down to Blanco, the steep walk down the broken road to the beach strewn with driftwood where whales swam staring wisely with calves and I'd found the will to live and not die.

DO NOT ENTER, the sign said.

Dying changed everything for Swimmer.

For one thing, not knowing how old you were or who was friend or foe, loved or hated, or whether or not you were a pacifist or a monk who'd forgone knowledge of the carnal body. What if you were a Republican, or a child molester for Christ's sake. Words and concepts came easily to him; he was amazed at how much he knew, as a river of insight had flown across the blank of his consciousness. Unusual facts came to him in a snap: the proper ratio of cucumber to yogurt in raita, that microwaves were radiation with wavelengths of 10^{-4} to one meter, the Wife of Bath's sadness and regret and finally all out love for the man who'd treated her the worst. He understood that the *Tao* that can be described is not the true *Tao*, which defied human logic. He loved life. He'd fallen in love with life, all of it. He made relatives of birds, mosquitoes, a wedge of lemon.

But regarding himself, Swimmer was blank. And there was something quite liberating about that holy not knowing—it allowed him to live in a way that felt, well, present. Even though all his therapy—save the lung work with the pulmonologist—was geared toward remembering, Swimmer secretly hoped all that he'd forgotten would stay wherever it had gone. He remembered neither sadness nor fear nor anything at all save contentment—maybe that's what dying was, a great forgetting?

"But what if you've never been accepted into the fold?" a Catholic priest objected during a counseling session. "Or what if forgetting somehow precluded heavenly father's bestowal of grace?"

Swimmer noted the nebular hypothesis for the priest, recounted the weak nuclear force of neutrinos. The old man grimaced.

He shook his head and fingered the silver cross, and who'd once been named Dare knew very well the purpose of a cross.

Doctrine was unclear in such matters.

His soul was in existential jeopardy, who they called Swimmer. Perhaps he'd hurtled back to the innocence of a child? Who could say?

Swimmer turned twenty and then twenty-one and though the breath still squished in his lungs, he made progress—at least his body did. He remembered water, the surf, how a rip hauls you at right angles and the way salt water sluiced through the mouth and teeth when breathing between strokes. It mostly all came back, in snippets and chunks, and by the time he made Coast Guard Rescue for Oregon's Southern Coast, it ceased to matter that he'd technically drowned and been revived. He trained hard, all swimmers did, and his first daytime rescue of a surfer in a wetsuit, washed out from a reef, was smooth and his voice had somehow calmed the target, put the man at ease. He'd ticked off the moves when the hoist dropped, buckled straps and tapped the top of his head three times—Swimmer's code for everything OK.

We backtracked north along the cliff trail through a heavy wood with no windows to the sea save the occasional flash of blue, so when we emerged from shadow the view waylaid us from every direction. The three of us sat on a bench no doubt placed on the spot for that very reason—how many had walked out of the deep dark wood and swooned at such a sight? Lara's breath caught. Professional photographs from this cliff face could be found everywhere. They littered the internet when summoned by name. I had one framed at home, the driftwood littered curve of beach stretching forever south along the blue blue water cut with foam. The place where the old me lay down and died, and the new one crawled up out of breaker and went on with life. The reproductions get something of the vastness of blue water, how it was possible to gaze out south to north, spin east and then back south and see nothing but the Pacific. It was as if the viewer hung suspended on a precipice overlooking some Cenozoic sea-world, and the neck of forest that fell down to the foot of surf where a triangular spire—Needle Rock, the first of the lighthouse keepers called it—rose simultaneously dark and light. Where, bifurcated by shadow to the north, a black and white boat hull just now shone from the teeth of shoal. Dead out there, bloated, a thing that didn't belong.

Low tide, a bulldozer hauled a trailer with a lashed down Honey Bucket, coils of wire and water jerries. It hummed up the strand of beach toward two trucks, one rigged with a winch on a steel rigging with a cable stretched out to where a diver in a wetsuit and flippers swam toward the wrecked boat's exposed side. Then appeared another black-clad man with a tool he proceeded to whomp hell out of the boat with—the sledge connecting mutely followed by metallic clangs. Bam, bam, bam. The toll reached us delayed by several heartbeats, the effect odd and beautiful.

"Dad," Lara said. "This is better than a movie."

She stretched out, her back to the green grass, as big as me, her mother's eyes. A trail wound down the bluffs to surf. Low tide, we watched the divers in wet suits hammer the ship's hull, stretch cables and tie them.

In the morning, at high tide, they'd try hauling her out.

The SAR alarm went off just after midnight. It was the morning of 21 July, a Tuesday, only an hour after he'd climbed into his bunk. A boat had hit rocks off Blanco, the engine room had flooded, they were going down that second. The rescue crew hit weather right off the bat, cliff winds, downdrafts. There was fog, a low ceiling. The copter's hoist malfunctioned. The pilot said get ready to swim. A lot.

Two hundred fifty yards in rescue gear, eight times, sea at seven, maybe ten feet. Swimmers prepare for this moment every day, the training pool with its fat fake waves, the sound of their parent sump pumps whirring underneath, Satan's own riptide barreling in at right angles.

"Him first," the captain said, pointed at the man hyperventilating in the life raft.

Swimmer'd shown him how to be taken hold of, how to stay clear. Swimming them in, he'd ridden the rip, another taking him back—four men, eight swims.

After, wrapped in blankets, the copter down on the beach now, he'd talked to them, the four rescued men. They talked of their wives and children, the holidays to come. One spoke of wolves howling from the edges of the great forest, how that sound had got into his dreams where once he was drowning, seeing the light of day through water, how it fell in spear shafts through the deep where wolves howled and up was down and down was up. They'd humped for shrimpers and longliners and codmen, knew their way around keel and bow, and to a man they'd seen bigger water than today. They'd all been overboard with sharks and cuda. But today was different. They weren't meant to make it. Today, Neptune had held aloft his trident and deemed them drown. Swimmer'd somehow interceded, cheated death of their mortal bodies.

Behind a counter in the Cape Blanco Lighthouse Greeting Center was an oldish man who knew and was not shy about revealing everything there was to know about the wreck, rescue and ongoing salvage of the Jamie K. Rumors were flying, he said when I tried to buy three five-dollar tickets for the lighthouse. Only, there'd been an engineering failure so entry was not allowed and thus the sweeping panoramic view from the tallest lighthouse on the furthest out piece of coastline in Oregon was off-limits, like the beach with its powdery dune, and everything else we'd come to see or do so far. Maybe nobody was supposed to see what they pulled out of that boat. Maybe the show was too good for the ticket. People were saying all kinds of things.

Who knew?

Outside the snug building the wind was gale force, thirty, forty knots sustained. A tour bus had parked at the gate and a whole tribe of old folk were chasing blown off hats to the edge of the abyss.

It had been a comedy of errors—that helicopter with its dead hoist twisting in the gale. Ten- thousand hillbillies camped up the road, blocking it for ten miles so God himself couldn't get in for nothing. Drank the liquor store dry, they did. Blue Moon, almost. At first it was thirty- thousand pounds of shrimp, then sixty; somebody claimed it was a drug boat full of high grade sinsemilla. Wacky weed. Hell, that swimmer, he'd saved their asses.

"Forgive me, ma'am," the geezer said, flashed that knowing look.

Renee'd found her way to the Guest Book, the very same one, it appeared, that we'd signed thirteen years ago, when death and drowning had been hard on us and I'd swum out to the very rocks the ship lay broken on now in salvage, screaming words that verged between rage and grief, this world and the hereafter, and she and Lara'd stood by the body of the bloated sea lion, fresh flowers laced into its mane for the trip ahead, and heard. They built a blue-doored shelter, gone inside. In time, I'd followed, lifted the blue door and lived.

I said. "*Lara.*"

On display in the room's center, opened to the very month, was the book itself, proof enough. It was the last thing on earth we'd expected. Lara, seventeen now, a woman now, she traced her name with a finger, her mother's, mine. Who we were then, three bound together on this fingernail of earth, hurting. Those people, they'd run out of earth to escape on, they were fried, up shit creek. I felt sorry for them, the way you feel sorry for someone who's died and doesn't know about some great good thing that happened later—a son finding his way through love, a granddaughter passing her driver's test after failing three times, the moment when the heart makes peace with loss and keeps beating. Tangled up with Swimmer's story, I'd learn, my own.

Later, we'd hide from the wind behind the lighthouse. I'd talk them into trespassing out to the forbidden hilltop crowned with its full-circle view. Wild opuntia grew at our feet. One of us would trip, split a fruit open, the bright pink flesh aroma washing over us. We'd lift our hands to protect eyes from wind and light and the dizzying distance beyond. This walk, it was totally forbidden, off-limits. Signs said trespassers would be prosecuted. There were fines, worse. We were not allowed to be on the ground where we'd soon walk, here, and this would make the vision sweeter—the tiny figures mute angels climbing from the wrecked ship and beyond.

With her finger she traced the loops of who we were then, very real words she'd forgotten ever having made, the summer she'd tromped a crude heart into the beach sand after her daddy'd burnt the calendar, drank hard whiskey, and swam into the sharp rocks. She was four years old then, a lifetime ago.

From the forbidden hilltop we'd witness the rescue, the broken fruit at our feet proof that we'd been there, caused our bit of damage and gone home.

Yonder

Yonder lifts his eyes to the predawn sky, and so witnesses the ancestral kill. Frost peppers his face. Above, lucent and true, Orion aims for the bull's red eye, the percussive whump ever rousing a dozing hunter from autumnal bed. O.W.'s exhaust still fumes the air. Half-a-mile gone, his headlights craze the pine tops down Starks-Bland Road. Yonder imagines dashlight on his old man's face, a whiff of gasoline from the hole in the engine block where the .30-ought six went off last night. The trail to Yonder's stand runs down into the rot beneath oak canopy, cut now and again by lobed cypress, the stray cedar and blackjack. November shiver in his spine, he sniffs the unborn morning, the flesh of antler-torn sapling splattered with deer piss. New frost crunches underfoot. Down and down, past Professor's persimmon and old Man Lyle's stand deluxe, with its new-cut plywood floor and pint bottle of Everclear under a stack of dew-stained Playboys. O.W.'s unpawned the guns again, the Model 11, sweet with WD-40 and lemon oil, loaded to the gills with number one buck alternated with magnum slugs. Yonder carries the gun by its stock, clicks the safety off and shoulders it a time or two. He picks his way. Night vision sharpens so he recognizes individual trees, deep-splayed hoofprints V-ing the mud. His tree stand, a homemade ten-footer, leans against a giant pin oak where the bottom opens between thicket and cutover. O.W.'s dangled a nylon rope from the seat platform. Yonder's supposed to loop the shotgun's pistol grip, hoist it aft once he's up, but hell with all that. Daylight's daylight. Opening Day, 1973, Weyerhauser land outside Carthage, Arkansas, he leans the gun in the crook of an arm, lifts one numb foot to the rung and climbs.

Back at Camp Fordyce, everything's got money laid on it: the exact minute of the first kill, the name of the dog to strike first scent, who'll have to haul down and take a country shit, who'll fall asleep and who'll wake up, the number of golden buzzards circling above when Lucian skins out camp meat, whether the stomach contents will herald cut acorn or crabapple as 73's forage of choice. Money's down on whose shirt tail gets cut off for missing a shot and who'll dip their face into the warm blood of a first kill. A pot's going on how long it'll take Dr. Clyde to get the game warden drunk, and who'll be first to catch Josephine Stepwell's wrath.

Gorney, the five-hundred-pound Razorback hog whose tusked grin shines on wanted posters hammered to Weyerhauser trees from here to kingdom come—he's got a hundred dollar bill riding on his head. TREE KILLING HOG WANTED DEAD, the bold print says.

Already on ice: a coon and brace of dove, two big-balled fox squirrels, a stringer of yo-yoed crappie Uncle Willard scored on the way down from DeGrey, twenty-five pounds of chopped pork butt and a bucket of Robert E. Lee's sop-sauce. A mess of greens and a sackful of tomatoes are crisping on the back porch, and one by one they've lardered butternut squash, onions, peppers, half a bushel of blue lake bush beans and a whole ham, and five gallons of almost apple jack in case a hard freeze comes. Cigars and whiskey and homemade wine, sandwich bologna and Josephine's opium, marked and unmarked playing cards, a whole shitload of Pabst Blue Ribbon from the Crossett distributor, and hooter, likely Professor's sitting on hooter stash, about to quote a ten-page poem about ducks. But none of this holds a rat's ass to fresh. Lucian, camp cook in even the oldest stories of Camp Fordyce, awaits first meat and there's where the heft of today's cashola lay—who'll bring down the tender hart for the old black man, whetting his ten-inch skinner.

Cold puts you square in the here and now.

Yonder sits his butt on the frosty platform, looks out on the blue-black morning. Here, this instant, his still hunt begins. He takes a breath, turns it loose and the cold comes on. His feet go first. The left boot's too tight so he's sweated during the walk down. The toes burn and tingle, then an ache climbs his leg, up under his long johns past his pecker and into his backbone. Yonder leans into his tree, shivers. He sweeps his eyes one-hundred-and-eighty degrees right to left. The sun will come up behind his back, in the eyes of the whitetail who belong to this wood, who slip in-between, show themselves to you in pieces and disappear. Whitetail knee-walking Arkansas brush, first light in the bottoms where the rutty buck snorts, steam rising. The earth waking from its smokey dream.

The cold gets up your nose.

It says, "Hey Jack, how you like them apples?"

It worms through your face into a molar nerve and there's not a goddamn thing Yonder can do about it. A still hunt's just that, still. It's about stretching a moment sideways so time and light and living things can pass through breathing, barely.

He blows warm breath into his trigger hand.

Yonder senses light, a rose-pink smidgen. The wood quakes into focus. Light enough to kill.

A ways off, gunshot booms. Yonder hears it, the lead hit meat. First kill—down.

He sweeps left to right, only moving his eyes. A shape halts in the periphery to his left, freezes, looks him straight through. She sees him as he sees her, a difference, something not there before.

"Kill a doe, I'll wrap at son-bitch round a tree," O.W.'d said, jabbing a finger at the Model 11.

Sometimes the buck will follow. He needs her nose, her keen eye to sweep the new-lit wood. Yonder is a blue eye to her, a wisp of breath rising from the tree trunk. He is white light, her mortal enemy—thirteen-year-old boy with his ass frozen to a piece of plywood.

She sees him and waits.

Yonder sits stone still. His heart pounds. Blood thumps in his inner ear. Every cell in his body says kill, lift weapon, cut throat, taste blood. The ape who fathered his kind is doing back flips, miming the story of blood sport with a jasper point laced to a willow stick. His breaths are ragged. His hands shake violently. Tears blur the vision.

The doe dips her head, swipes a mouthful of dead grass and passes. She flicks her white tail and trots, leaps an eight-foot bramble. She keeps her shoulder to the thicket where her mate snorts, the slightest flash of horn tines. Not five minutes into daylight and Yonder's been spotted. Squirrels bark out the word; directly, crow will write Yonder's name in the sky.

Buck fever passes. Cold air seeps into his eyeballs. Yonder is laid open to the wood.

Somewhere behind his back is the monster he feared beneath his bed on childhood nights when tornado sirens howled, when the wind came and Ozone in the air smelled like burnt skin and green light flickered on the windowpane. Another gunshot, then a third. A fourth. Many years hence, as an old man, he'd trade his life for a shot of this daylight, for an inch of its thorny grain. There is no crack of dawn—what a crock. Dawn is like a wood-fire started with bone and spindle. When the punk catches, thin smoke rises. But where does bone end and fire begin?

A Walker dog yelps over to Adair Road.

Josephine's TV said this spaceship named Mariner blasted off from earth yesterday, headed for the inner solar system—Venus and Mercury and the sun, should it fly that far, out there shining. I'll be damned, go to hell, Yonder thinks. A wedge of ducks flies over quack-quacking, pink sunlight on their whistling wings. The sky is baby blue, sweet and tender, the lone morning star fading on the horizon.

Hunter's taught him not to wear gloves, not even the cheap ass K-Mart kind O.W. wears. Hands are uppity, forget them. Whitetail can see you from his sleep, from a million miles away, he knows what you think, what you dream. He knows if you jack off in the top bunk like Preacher Mann does when Uncle Willard's sawing logs and everyone's supposed to be asleep. He knows you're here to kill, just like you did in the beginning with that poisoned arrow that touched his lung while you tracked him through the bloody snow. He saw you kill his mama. Saw you field dress her to warm your frozen fingers, cut out the liver, name it sweetbread, lift to the mouth, and eat. He suspects, vaguely, a dish called Brains and Eggs. He knows the ape in your heart, the blood lust, the whole nine yards.

Gold light strums through the limbs, warm on Yonder's face. Behind his back, the underbrush cracks. Faint movement prickles his neck hairs. Maybe the wood has him in her sights, his blaze orange hat in the crosshairs. A silver creek thrusts into a brier patch, back there where wild animals sluice mud over tongues for salt. Hunter's taught him to turn his head away from what he needs to see. A cave man trick, Hunter says, passed down from the days of old, when our kind dodged the starved saber-tooth, big fucker crouched in shadows with six-inch fangs. In low light, the corner of the eye sees intensely. Holy sight, Hunter calls it, save your ass. Stalking wood or dead-on still hunt, look away, Yonder. Hunter practices what he preaches, never looks you in the eye. Bent hard right, Yonder's neck cracks. Whatever's behind him stills.

The dogs go off in a glorious howling.

Two kinds of deer dog in the Arkansas woods: Walkers and Beagles. A Walker dog's rawboned long and lean, sweet-mouthed with Jesus's own nose. Greyhound fast, he'll run a deer to death. His bark is a rhythmic baritone. If a Walker's on, best brace on a tree, click the safety off and lay finger to trigger. Prepare for shit to hit the fan. Beagles, what Old Man Lambert runs, are another story. They're happy lolly-gaggers, short legged-yowlers, who couldn't run a deer down to save their lives. But they'll stay on the scent, yip-yapping, and let the deer slip in front, no rush, no hurry, take your time. And it's beagles Yonder hears this second, the high-pitched yelps of one Lambert calls Jim Bowie, after the knife he ever wears on his hip—Arkansas toothpick, he'll say, smile that toothless peckerwood grin.   So Bowie's got his noseful. Poon-Tayne, Sassy and Biscuit Lip join in with the others, a mile as crow flies, Yonder guesses. They choir the Weyerhauser lands, the chase full-on now, a song like knives singing over the Dallas County bottoms.

O.W.'s bought these little plastic bottles of doe piss at the outdoor supply. They come in a cardboard box with a drawing of a grinning buck mounting a doe. "Make that buck crazy for you," the bubble dialogue says: *Every Drop Produced By A Living Animal In Estrous!* And that's exactly how it smells, like tired-old-worn-out deer piss. How is it a grown man can douse you with such? What was O.W. thinking? What event, exactly, was he trying to precipitate? That's what Yonder's thinking when Gorney walks smack out of the woods, right out in front of the tree stand, close enough to hit with a rock.

A great beagle crescendo passes over Starks-Bland Road and into the wood, rolling toward him and this hog that's big as a buffalo, eyes ablaze and hide bristling. How it seems to thirteen-year-old Yonder on Opening Day, with the new sun filtering through tree limb, beagles burning down the hill, the whole world shining.

Gorney lifts snout as if posing for the WANTED—TREE KILLING HOG poster, so Yonder sees the yellow sheen on both tusks, big gnashing teeth grown curving out of a crooked mouth. The hog hisses and snorts, looks up at Yonder like they're old friends. *Snorka, snorka*, he says, *gomp, gomp.* Gorney does not appear bothered in the least by the presence of a boy holding a twelve-gauge scatter-gun. *Morning, son,* Gorney says. *Taken you long enough.* The eyes are dark and knowing, human-looking, like they've seen a thing or two. Gorney snuffles the air. *Why you squirted down wid deer piss, boy? Say?* His breath steams out, reeks of acorn, turnip root, muscadine.

Three distinct rifles boom that second and the dogs lay into whatever the hunters have missed. A quarter mile off and hauling ass. Yonder hears tree branches crack. The morning transpires. In his whole sorry-ass life, O.W. could not have foretold this. The enormous hog snorts steamy breaths beneath the tree stand where Yonder sits transfixed. He lifts both ragged ears, looks the boy in the eye. *Let's talk turkey, Owen.*

Yonder's never talked to a hog, much less one who could speak his Christian name. He'd once met a woman whose wiener dog could say *Elvis* but this hog's a whole different deal.

"How you know my name?"

Gorney scratches one ear with a hind hoof, his bristly coat mottled with shades of earth. His countenance is familiar—Yonder's seen this pig somewhere before, and not just on Weyerhauser posters. Gorney looks up at the boy. The boy looks down at Gorney.

The hog sighs. *You known me,* he says. *I ripped your rompers on the Kaldony field. Tweren't I give you that mark?* Gorney turns toward the coming of the dogs. His growl is monstrous, a dragon snarl, each yellow-scummed tusk the shining length of Lucian's butcher knife.

Yonder traces the scar on his thigh as a rifle repeats, the old ache.

Deadwood breaks a hundred yards in front of the dogs who're squalling and yelping and pissing themselves for the joy of chase. What goddamn fun. Yonder sees sunshine glance off the buck's rack. An eight point, maybe ten, vine like a vernal crown strung through the tines and trailing. He's loping through the new-lit wood, white tail flagging.

Yonder clicks safety off and the buck freezes. It snorts loudly, noses the air and looks straight at Gorney, then up at the boy on the stand. The tableaux is complete. Lambert's beagles are in sight now, Jim Bowie with Poon-Tayne at his tail.

The sun looks more like bone than fire. A bundle of mistletoe shimmies high in the pin oak above, a mess of white berries poison and divine. The here and now shines in the periphery. Backlit by gauzy sunshine, three wood-nymphs dance with a holly-crowned faun. Goat-eyed Bacchus bleats from the briers and an Ivory Bill screams *Pan! Pan! Pan!*

The trigger makes of Yonder its cold demand.

When he shoots, the big-racked buck lopes beyond the clearing and disappears into the caney breaks. The dogs never miss a lick, they run by nose to the ground, their little red dog peters unfurled. Opening Day, they're free for the chase. The sun has risen and they've struck scent—the thunderous rifles have sung praise. Past Professor's persimmon and Old Man Lyle's stand deluxe, they've run the buck to the edge of a deep, dark wood where the water is cold for the lapping and they will lay down in the shade of an evergreen. The lady will rise from the water with good meat to fill their dream bowls and the sloe-eyed nymphs will scratch their backs with sharp nails.

Gorney lay on his side in a puddle of blood. The gun powder smell is sharp, a puff of white smoke rising from the vent-ribbed barrel. Lambert's dogs break off toward Adair Road. The eight-point's home free. Yonder looks at the frost-strewn ground. The hog is beautiful, a god or something, and now he's gone and killed it. Killed god. Why'd he done that? Gorney's his row to hoe, now.

Yonder loops the shotgun's pistol grip, lowers the thing. People have blown their heads off this way, messing with guns on ropes. Only not this time, she lay down pretty at the ladder foot. Yonder's numb from the waist down. By the time he makes the bottom rung, needles prick each foot.

The view's all different from down here. Yonder unloops the Model 11. The barrel's hot. Three rounds remain in the magazine, a live slug in the chamber. He clicks the safety off, feels eyes behind his back. What before had been a panorama is now cutover littered with nickel-sized acorns that slip-slide beneath his boot soles.

He approaches the fallen hog.

The sun's at Yonder's back, in the talker pig's eyes. Gunshots echo far and near. A fox squirrel barks from a sweetgum as Hurricane Creek coils into the thicket. Yonder walks a wide swath around the hog—the head alone big as the hood of O.W.'s truck. A fist-size hole in Gorney's shoulder oozes. This close, he can smell the thing—musky and pungent, the smell of cottonmouth, scum dripping down the foot-long tusks.

Yonder leans the Model 11 against a black jack.

The eyes are open, warm and familiar. Steams rises from the snout. "I'm sorry about this, Gorney," Yonder says, kicks one scuffed hoof.

Yonder buries a boot toe in Gorney's butt—and the hog explodes. He thrusts his awful snout upward, twists a shining tusk through Yonder's right thigh. The light changes. A lid of cloud slides over the sun. Warm blood sloshes into Yonder's rubber boot. He kicks away from the hog, drags himself to the rooty cradle where the shotgun leans. Then, back to the tree, he shoulders the gun and fires four times wildly.

This close, a blind boy could hit a hog with a slug.

Later, after they've drug him and Gorney from the wood, after the ceremonial cutting off of shirt tails and blood lettings, after the feast of fresh meat topped off with Rocky Mountain Oysters, when the men sink into low chairs with their whiskeys neat before the stone hearth, when Doc has sewed him back together and Josephine's shared her yellow medicine, he'll be asked to tell the story, Yonder, to add his puny voice to the age-old fray.

"You ought not to've done that," he tells the dead hog, no answer, save *boom-boom-boom* from the deep dark wood.

Leviathan: Monster of the Deep

The Super 8's across the road from Knight's Grocery, where I once paid to see a gray whale floated in a semi-trailer full of formaldehyde. Behind the check-in counter, a wall clock has Hari Krishna written in red across its white face. The Indian owner has never looked me in the eye, always the aroma of coriander and tumeric and toasted cumin rich in the lit-up lobby. She's taken off her *hajib* since our last visit—the red dot floating between her eyes. "Your father, Mr. Harvell. We have two messages."

Out in the Pathfinder, Renee and Lara sit with the air on high. It's hot as hell, you forget a pain like heat. Asphalt mirages shimmer over the hotel parking lot. Renee's had to pee since Carlisle.

One note, written in the hostess's precise hand says *Joey, Key on top of electric box. Gone to get haircut. Judy and Bold flying down. O.W.* Next is a hand I've seen him write into the IceLand Driver's Log on Sundays after a heavy meal. He'd be about to hit the road—eastbound in an IceLand rig—forging his eight hours on, eight hours off across Tennessee and North Carolina, hauling ten tons of slaughter turkeys. *Viewing tomorrow afternoon,* O.W.'s written on the Super 8 note pad.

"122," the hostess says. "At government rate. Bottom floor. How many nights?" Children laugh behind the wondrous smelling door.

"We've had a death in the family."

We've never really talked about anything but extra towels—the Indian hostess and me—but I've watched her children grow from babies—there's something to say for that. "I don't know how long we'll be here."

She passes card keys. "As long as you require. Our ice machine is out. We're sorry."

I stick my head out one of the double glass doors, yell 122 to Renee, and point east. Lara's already tumbled from our renegade Pathfinder, joyously swinging open the pool deck gate. A cedar gazebo's been built across the lawn; sun shines through the lattice work.

The hostess lights a stick of incense beneath the Krishna clock, disappears through the family door. She's remembered Mama's state discount, has interacted with O.W. He's stood in this very spot, breathing, the air hissing a little over the front tooth I chipped for him on the day *Leviathan* came.

Uncle Bold and Aunt Judy drive up while I've got Lara Super 8 poolside, Renee off buying enough vodka to kill a horse. Judy's O.W.'s sister, who years ago exiled herself the hell out of Arkansas for Baltimore, Maryland and a good-hearted Pole named Bold Dujenski. They get out of a silver rental under the check-in awning. Bold recognizes me straight away, waves a big hand as Lara cannonballs off the shallow end ledge. They leave both doors open. For a second it seems a remarkable coincidence—us here at the same time.

Bold says, "We're floored. I'm so sorry, Jimmy."

"Joey," I say.

Judy hugs me over the pool fence. She's crying. "We've got to stop meeting like this," she says.

Fifteen years ago they'd walked into the Washington D.C. restaurant where I waited tables to tell me Jimmy'd died. In walked Uncle Bold and Aunt Judy, a lively Friday crowd crowing through the tail end of lunch. Bold said, "Where's the men's room, Jimmy?" Inside, Uncle Bold put a hand on my shoulder. "Your brother's dead," he said. Only he got the names bass-akwards, as he ever had since I'd known him. "Jimmy," he said and looked me straight in the eye. "Joey's dead. He died in a car wreck last night."

Lara drips beside me. Honeysuckle's in the air.

"She's beautiful," Judy says. "Where's Renee?"

"Buying liquor."

"Good," Bold says and shakes out a cigarette.

Judy says, "What's your name, honey?"

Lara giggles behind my back. The sun feels good. "Tell her your name."

She says, "Lara."

"Little lovely Lara."

Judy looks rough, like somebody who's traveled a long way for a funeral.

"Ask the hostess for government rates. She'll know what you're talking about."

Judy hugs me again and this time I smell she's been drinking. "Have you spoken to O.W.?" Bold puts his hand on her shoulder.

"No. I haven't."

Lara and I are eating road food when Renee walks in. We've showered, taken a walk around the parking lot perimeter where road-dusty blackberries are going purple. My mouth is salty. I mean to say that my mouth tastes like I've gnawed a salt block all 1077.3 miles from Melbourne Beach, Florida up to Lonoke, all those miles of grit between my teeth. Renee's bought barbecue sandwiches from Mean Pig, baked beans and potato salad, a plastic half-gallon of Popov Vodka.

"Bold and Judy are here."

"Here?"

"Here."

"Where?"

"Out there. They've got a room."

"What did O.W. say?"

"Nothing."

"What?"

"I didn't call yet."

"Well you better." Renee starts unpacking the watery cooler into our mini-fridge. "You should. Right now."

Lara's cartoon is *Power Puff Girls*, these super heros from second grade or something who're beating the Jesus out of some poor bad guy. "Help," he says. "*Enough, enough*," he cries. Lara screams when I click the TV off, as if I've committed violence.

Renee says, "Hell, Joey."

On a chair outside the front door, out in the humid night, cicadas make that ratchet noise that gets under your fillings. Across the street, a snow cone vendor does business where the whale was once parked. A bare bulb shines—I can see his head.

Renee's tired. "Joey," she says through the window. "Call."

How must O.W. have felt fifteen years ago when the dispatchers radioed that Mama was waiting at the terminal. That she was a wreck. That something awful had happened and he needed to skip his remaining drops, get home A.S.A.P. Dead-heading across Tennessee through Nashville and Memphis, the glass pyramid at river bridge and that long stretch of earth between places. Then Mama said Jimmy was dead and he got that look on his face—half surprise, half something else. *Jimmy*, his blood son's name—how long did that word take to sink in?

I call.

Only instead of O.W., it's Mama, her voice on the answering machine, and I don't expect that, not for a second, her sweet words telling me in that way she can't make get to the phone right now, that if I'll leave my message at the sound of the beep, she'll get back to me soon as she can. Just to hear her, I try again. And again. Until finally her voice is gone, just silence, empty space.

A car drives up across the street and two girls order cones. The vendor had enough ice for a zillion vodka tonics—enough to float a whale like the dead grey that lay over there in 1985. This was the Dixie circuit—it was nothing for a Peterbilt to pull off the interstate with a six-hundred-pound rat, two-headed goats or Donkey Woman nursing horsey-faced twins. *Leviathan's* arrival coincided with our first fistfight—mine and O.W.'s—the one we had just before Jimmy died. We'd all been driving back from having a family photograph in Little Rock, Trace and Jimmy in the backseat of the blue Cougar, me up front with Mama—O.W. driving. I was twenty-four that summer, living home again from school, bar hopping nights and finishing concrete days. Mama's lupus had just kicked in, barely, just barely. Me and Jimmy'd gone out drinking the night before the scheduled sitting. In Jacksonville, we got pretty shit-faced at a cowboy bar— which was my fault— and danced with Air Force women until two in the morning. O.W.'d smelled it on my breath. He'd glowered all morning and I'd glowered back. I was serious about not taking any guff from anybody by then, especially O.W. Earlier that fall, Sophomore year U.A., after he'd got wind of the DWI, he showed up out of the blue to take my car away. On my desk he found a copy of a Chinese Folk Tale book named *Monkey*. He'd jabbed a finger at the cover where this picture of a monkey had *Monkey* written in big black letters across its head.

"That's says we come from Monkeys, don't it."

Before I could say no, that it was about these Chinese people who were poor and lived on the hard earth just like us, O.W. threw *Monkey* across my desk, took the keys to my blue Cutlass and drove off down Highway 71 to Lonoke. No *goodbye* or *kiss my ass* or *your mama's worried about you*, nor anything at all. Maybe I felt sorry for myself. Did he remember the railroad tracks, how his head bled all down the back of his white shirt—the one with *O.W.* written on the heart side of his chest? That time he'd walked away and left us there.

The Cougar had power windows and I'd rolled mine down. O.W. rolled it up. "The air's on," he said.

"I want fresh."

"Tough," he said.

I said, "Fuck you, O.W."

He let the car coast onto the highway curb. "*Joey*," Mama said.

"Do *what*?" O.W. said.

"*St-st-stop* this," Jimmy said. Traceleen sat white-faced.

"I said fuck you. Fuck you, O.W. Hey Jimmy? Trace? Anybody ever tell you about how I lay in bed one night listening to him beat hell out of Mama. She said, 'Joey, get help. He's killing me. Joey, *please*."

Mama said, "That's enough, Joe."

"He *was* killing you, Mama. You know it."

O.W. met me at the passenger door. And we fought one another out under a blue sky between soy fields where lazy crop dusters dumped poison on summer soy. It was the sort of day when boys oblivious to their own deepening voices fished pond banks, sometimes forgetting for a night the sunfish lashed on makeshift stringers, so that when the line was retrieved next day a water moccasin writhed where fish should be, and the shock would be gut-level so they'd never forget to suspect duplicity in all things. Though the fight was quick, I managed a left hook that broke one of O.W.'s front teeth and split my knuckle. He got this *I didn't know you'd do that* look on his face, blood running down his lip.

"You woodpussy," he said, and knocked my breath out.

And for the rest of it, the whole time while he kicked my ass, patches of blue sky shone through the cracks where wrist-thick snakes writhed on summer lines, I remember thinking *woodpussy*? What the hay was *woodpussy*?

The big gray was the first whale me or Jimmy'd ever seen, coated in a slick layer of cottage cheese looking stuff. It just lay there. No posters of living whales or Shamu with a beach ball on his nose or instruction on how to behave in such a beast's presence. Just a big, fat Leviathan: Monster of the Deep in a stinking trailer, getting hauled through towns like ours, a skinny boy barking off the wooden platform below the monster sign. Leviathan's arrival was an annual deal. Somehow it'd got out that the thing was some kind of conduit to the spirit world, so everybody and their mama came to stand in line. People'd show up at Knight's Grocery on Friday and cash their paychecks, wait their turn in the parking lot.

Jimmy pointed at my duct-taped knuckle. "That thing needs p-peroxide. Is it true?"

"What?"

"You know."

"It happened. You weren't born yet."

"Bu-bullshit." My brother spat. "You dreamed it."

"She laid his cheek open with her fingernail. You know the scar."

"Shit," Jimmy said.

"These idiots believe it t-talks to dead people."

A lady up ahead of us kneeled at the whale's head. She'd got down on her hands and knees, put her mouth up close to one of the filmy eyes. "Daddy?" she was saying. "Can you hear me? *Daddy?* Are you listening?"

Jimmy said. "Who'd p-pay for that?"

I said, "Us."

The woman on her hands and knees was crying—the grief was hard on her, you could tell. I wondered what I'd have to say to the whale's head when my time came. I was thinking about the other-worldly feel of getting your ass kicked, how Mama's face looked like inside the car—how on a railroad track she'd hummed this song called *The Moon Over Naples.* Blue Traceleen in her church dress. And I was thinking how it was to have a brother, to see him grow up to be number 86, right defensive end for the State Championship Jackrabbits of 1985, to watch him throw forearm shivers and sing in the church choir on Sunday, then walk out the big double doors they'd so soon carry his casket through, six-feet tall and sawdust bronze—that was Jimmy. I loved him.

Outside, somebody racked off muffler glass-packs—O.W.'s Chevy, sounded like.

The woman cut us a hard look—she glared straight through us. Then she turned back to the whale, put her lips to the fetid face and kissed. "I know. I know you didn't mean to, Daddy. I fergid you."

It was embarrassing, the whale's big eyes like greasy saucers. "That lady's *b-bonko,*" Jimmy said, "Calling that thing daddy."

I'd get my answer. In the hallway before Mama's funeral. Both of us dressed up again, darkening the full-length mirror he'd screwed to the end wall. Just like before, her between us. Life is both brute and healer, the real son of a bitch. All my life I'd dreamed of breaking O.W.'s bones, of knocking teeth out of his head—and what kind of way was that for a son to think about its daddy? Once my wife asked, "How on earth can you love that man?" and the edge of my defense shocked.

"How can you love anybody?" I demanded. And my question stands.

"Can I ask you something? O.W.?"

"Shoot," he said.

"What's woodpussy?"

"What?"

"Woodpussy."

The solemn look melted, and he was just him, O.W., a man who'd given Mama a loaf of white bread from his delivery truck on the day they met. Who'd taught me the correct blade angle to whet a knife, how to pack a suitcase.

He said through a smile, *"Woodpussy?"*

"Yea."

"Remember all those antelope?"

I'd first seen the western states from the passenger side of his long-nose Peterbilt, the time he'd kidnapped me, sort of, to get mama back after the railroad track mess. "That place I took you, Highway 80 outside Rawlins?"

"Wyoming. By the prison. All those men in orange."

"You got it. There's this aspen grove up on a hilltop I drove through oncet. Somebody'd carved these tree burls into woman-shaped things. They leaked red sap. Like a woman on her moon. Weirdest things you ever saw, woodpussies."

We'd again follow the state trooper up to Solgahatchia, stand heat-stunned on fake grass, shield eyes against the blazing white casket and pray, pray, pray. Hear the click-click-click of the pulleys down. An evil aunt would say, "Why aren't you crying, boy?"

"Well why aren't you?"

The Seventh Direction

Set against the framework of their lives, *our* lives, that winter break when I was twelve was probably the high-water mark for them, Mama and O.W. They'd recovered as best they could from the house fire, Daddy'd got straight, with seniority at Continental Trailways, which put him in place to bid on the sort of charter trips that Mr. Cedric Lord wanted to New York City, Niagara Falls, and then Detroit, where a concluding dinner had been reserved at the famous revolving tower. I was halfway through sixth grade then, and we'd moved from the cold water shack in back of Uncle Earl's cow pasture to Lonoke, where they'd finagled a rent-to-own with space for Shawnee and a barn, a Kentucky wood fence encircling all on a sharp curve drunks missed some nights, so we'd wake up some mornings and find their smashed cars smoldering. Mama and Daddy'd both been saved at the Lonoke First Baptist Church Spring Revival, and Jesus had accompanied us into the new house with its garden spot and two-acre front yard. And then there was the trip, which Mama—I'm sure it was her—had prevailed upon O.W. to ask Mr. Cedric for his permission for me to go. We'd be gone for Christmas, but so what? I deserved the opportunity after what we'd been through. It was decided, my name was added to the roster. I'd have a seat on the bus, and share a hotel room with O.W. A Broadway ticket was agreed to, and a place at the table for the revolving tower finale.

Surely I had a suitcase, surely. And it would have been packed with the clothes given to me by the church after the house fire, husky corduroys that were too short, and print shirts that were always tight, so that even to this day I'll only wear extra-large, though my wife insists on buying large, so there's always the returns after Christmas, stacks on my dresser with a note that says, you do it, Mr. Big.

The night before we left, she came into my room, Mama. She was pregnant, I think, with Traceleen, and there would be complications, though none of us knew that then. "He'll be good to you," she said, and handed me a folded up twenty. "You be good back."

It had snowed, and this Canadian air had flown down and froze our pond thick enough to ride a horse over, so you could see eighty-pound Buffalo Carp swimming underneath, these six-foot shadows darting away from the cracks that zinged from Shawnee's hooves.

"I will," I said.

She ruffled my hair, hugged me to her chest. "I know you will, sweetie." I don't know what day of the week it was, or if we had a Christmas tree or a fire or any of that, but I remember the night before leaving, turning over and over, the sounds of the settling house and cars steering the curve out front. It took forever, all night.

But the next day came, and we drove the thirty miles to Little Rock under a bright Solstice sun, and the bus was ready when we got to the station, catered with a refrigerator unit loaded with cold cuts, cheese in velvety slices, bunches of grapes and tangerines, coarse mustards and mayonnaise, cakes, pastries, every kind of soda known to man including NuGrape and Fanta Orange, my favorites. Lights glowed from one end of the aisle to the other, and the diesel purred beneath us. There was the smell of cleanness on top of cleanness, cedar something, as I took a seat behind the driver's cab. In the four-foot wedge of rearview appeared O.W.'s face, his blue-eyed gaze that froze me to the core. "Get up," he said. "You know your number."

Big Cedric had arranged for the party to be picked up at Pleasant Valley Country Club where most of them were members, this green rolling golf course with the biggest houses on earth, it seemed to me, built right into it. The clubhouse itself was a mansion, with a drive under passage for valet service, a black man dressed in a coat and tie at the door, where out issued the couples who'd be my fellow travelers, men and women who regularly appeared on the Democrat-Gazette's Society Page, though how could I have known that then? O.W. rolled right up to valet parking, stepped down the short stairs, and shook hands with a man who held a notepad in one hand, reading glasses down his nose. Beside him was a short fat kid in Hushpuppies, little Cedric, his son.

Their suitcases arrived on a wheeled dolly, and it was O.W.'s job to load them into the belly of the bus, where already lay our puny luggage. The difference in Mr. Lord, standing there making marks on the yellow legal pad, and my father cannot be overstated. Mama'd married O.W., in part, I'd learn, because no one would ever fuck with him in a million years. Six feet one and two-forty, he looked more heavy weight prize fighter than bus driver, even in the clean pressed pants and razor creased shirt, a blue coat with the Continental Trailways Senior Driver badge pinned on it, a military style hat with its black bill shining. He took the coat off, and when he lifted a bag his muscles bulged. He was strong and fit, with a fierce blue in his eyes, so from my window seat in front of the bathroom I could see more than one of the fancy ladies with their cashmere sweaters look him up and down, then smile at each other, demure and white teeth straight behind red lipstick. Rich people are like that, not afraid to look.

Before noon, the charter bus with its crushed velour seats and cedar aroma had filled and departed, and as we headed out Highway 40 past the Lonoke Exit toward Memphis, bare soy fields and cotton growing straight up to the front doors of the folk who farmed it, Big Cedric—whose seat was the one where I'd mistakenly sat—stood up beside O.W. and spoke into the driver's microphone.

He said, "*Bon voyage* from the bridge."

"*Bon voyage*," the party said back. The seat beside me was empty, the armrest down. Someone was in the head already, I could hear them grunting.

"As we make our way to Memphis on the Mississippi, in the good hands of our driver, Captain Harvell, our lunch bar will open, and you will find that we have not spared on fare."

"Here, here, Bob," an invisible man said.

"When's happy hour," said another.

"It's 5 o'clock somewhere," added the red lipped women who'd eyed O.W.

Mr. Lord said, "That is the most important question I've heard all day." He waited for their clapping to stop, then added, "Serve yourself by seats, starting at the front and moving back."

The bathroom toilet made the swishing sound, and out came the fat kid who was Lord's son. With him came the smell. He looked at me.

"We have a full bar, Stoly for vodka and Wild Turkey for bourbon drinkers. *Laphroig* for single malt fans not afraid of peat. There's Boodles and Tanqueray, aperitifs and brandy, three top tier cognacs, Belgium beer and cases of *Poulet Foussey* and *Liebfrumilche* respectively. Two or three good reds in there to boot. *Lassiez les bon temps rouler*."

"*Lassiez les bon temps rouler*," the party said in unison.

And then commenced the first full-fledged rich people on the road party I'd ever in my life witnessed, so that by the time we crossed the Memphis river bridge, with the brown Mississippi shining below, a whole bunch of them were shit-faced, hitting the bathroom whose reek, I'd soon learn, can take on a personality all its own.

Captain Harvell, I was thinking, what was that?

This was not the first time I'd traveled cross country by bus. Two years earlier we'd ridden from Little Rock to Los Angeles, where we stayed with Mom Dee's people and went to Disneyland for one whole day. O.W.'s run was Oaklawn then—a daily charter to the racetrack in Hot Springs where the thoroughbreds raced every spring and a revelry of drunken gamblers made the hour-long commute by bus. There was the Arkansas Derby and an Easter race, McClard's barbecue with hushpuppies and tamales leftover that found its way to our house, this huge wood frame with two pastures we'd hayed the year before. Coming off their first divorce and reconciliation, the rent house with its muscadine vines and space for horses was his peace offering, I guess. Jimmy and I shared this whole upstairs floor big as the whole house. There was a window at one end, and a window at the other—about a football field away, or that's how it seemed when I was ten and the fire dream had come on me, so I talked to Jimmy about rigging a rope swing from our window to the big pecan outside—we'd swing free of the flames. He was five, towheaded, stuttering a little already.

Uncle Earl said that six sisters had shared our upstairs bedroom, and that one had got sick and died, so her ghost was in one of the closets that lined either side of the room from one end to the other. We kept a light on, always, me and Jimmy, and only opened the closets when he peed his bed. We'd stash the sheets in there, with the dead sister's ghost.

He started coming home buzzed, O.W.

Mama was expert at sniffing this out, she'd learned from Grandfather Si the lessons of detecting drunkenness, how a drinker'd tend to over enunciate instead of slur, the flushed face, a tendency toward the bathroom. It had all happened before, when they'd bowled on a league at Pleasure Lanes, and he'd got hit in the head with a tire tool one night in a brawl, so they'd screamed at each other on the way home, and O.W.'d killed the Pontiac on the train track, pulled the key, and walked away with the headlights shining on his back where head blood streamed down his white shirt, the one with his initials sewed into the heart side of his chest. Mama'd found a hideout key, drove us home, only he kicked the door down, and they'd gone at it in the bedroom next to mine. Maybe I remembered it all wrong, maybe I still do. But I don't think so. There was Christmas in hiding, when he'd broken the cop's jaw who delivered divorce papers. The tinfoil Christmas tree remained after they took him to jail, and I remember taking the gifts and putting them in the trunk of the car, and we'd driven to Mama's friend's house who had a minor bird named Polly who could say "goddamn." "Son of a bitch." "Kiss my ass."

We got past all that, it was in the past.

And then he started coming home to the big wood house buzzed and we'd eat our supper on TV trays in the living room, and one night Uncle Earl's friend John Timmerette did a doughnut in the front yard behind the wheel of a red Corvette and daddy'd lost it. Jimmy'd and I'd heard them all go at it down below, Mama's voice the highest, her saying *don't, don't,* so Jimmy'd repeat it, *d-don't, d-don't.*

The tickets were free, to LA and Disney Land, they were part of his privilege. Which was good because he'd started losing his paychecks at Oaklawn, that too. Uncle Earl'd slaughtered six smallish hogs and stored them in the chest freezer in our back room, only the motor'd shorted so the meat was rotting. The last thing Mama said to him on the way out to the station was "Take care of that meat. Get it out."

On the way back from our two-week trip, the Ft. Smith driver let it slip that the house had burned to the ground. He thought Mama knew. But she didn't. So the driver wouldn't say another word. And she'd burst into tears when he was standing there waiting for us in his crisp uniform under a blinking *Good Times Tulsa* sign.

They'd sifted the ashes with a piece of screen, looking for who knows what.

We lived in Uncle's back pasture shack for a while. Then came Lonoke, and another new beginning. And Mama was pregnant with my little sister. It was Christmas time and we were headed for New York City, me and my adoptive father, O.W., who'd made it out of our house on fire with only his underwear.

Fat Boy's name was Cedric, too. He missed his mother, who'd stayed home to have Christmas with his sister and the rest of the Lord household, which evidently included an elderly grandmother and grandfather who lived in the guesthouse, servants, a lawnsman, gardener, tutor, and chef. A French *au pair* had taught him French. His voice carried from midway up the aisle lit by tiny red lights, through some of the seats with reading lights on, over the snores of passed out revelers, to me, just in front of the bathroom with its little sign that alternated between occupied and vacant, the former red and the latter green. We'd climbed through Tennessee, headed north on 81, skirting the Appalachians into Virginia. The darling of the lady with bright red lipstick, Cedric, he was sitting with her, refilling her red wine a few times, and I learned about the school play where he got to be Joseph to a pretty blonde Mary, and she'd required him to kiss her to make the union real. The girl'd had to stuff a Winnie the Pooh doll up inside her dress so it looked like baby Jesus was in there, and one of the wise men had farted out loud during a scene and blamed it on his camel.

"And what was the kiss like," the lady with bright red lips who'd smiled at O.W. said. "Did she slip you the tongue?"

That's when he said he missed his mother, little Cedric, and they got quiet and maybe fell asleep.

Outside, the dark world flew by. I unfolded the letter and read again about how Mama and Jimmy were sending me heart messages that second, how I was to send a post card soon as we hit New York City, to brush my teeth and say "yessir" and "no mam." We'd turned a corner, our family, and from here it was all *up, up, up.* Say my prayers—they were real and could make a difference. Be sweet to daddy. He's trying hard. She said *Love You!* with an exclamation mark, Mama.

I missed her.

O.W. drove all night.

That's how I remember it, the sun coming up on a truck stop parking lot just outside of Maryland, tired-eyed company filing in for a sit-down breakfast while O.W. fueled, whacked bus tires with a metal tipped knocker, then had me wipe down the bathroom with Mr. Clean, a picture of a bald-headed man with big muscles on the label. Once inside, we sat with the other drivers, in a booth with a payphone hooked up to it, where he dialed Mama. The time had changed—we were an hour later, which seemed strange to me, being in a different zone than Mama and Jimmy, who'd thought that up?

"Mornin," O.W. said. "We're in Maryland."

Outside the window, the big bus shone, fueled, loaded to the gills with sandwich meat and pastry, enough liquor to kill twenty horses. Back in his drinking days O.W. used to take me to bars where men played shuffleboard, sprinkling sawdust on lathed wood tables. He'd order me a coke, sprinkle salt in his mug of beer, drop in a few peanuts and light a Pall Mall. Him and Uncle Earl stole some rope from a dump one time, and drove to a bar after where the cops showed up, *the man*, daddy called them.

He looked at me. "Yea, he's here."

Over the phone, her voice, enjoy my pancakes, do everything I can to help. Had I made friends with Mr. Lord's son yet? He was my age. He could be my friend. Love you, bye.

"All downhill from here," O.W. said. "I love you, too."

A waitress brought our food, pancakes, sausage and bacon and ham and hash browns and grits, O.W.'s four eggs over-easy and mine scrambled, a chicken fried steak with white gravy and hand cut fries, coffee and orange juice. And to top it all off, Mr. Lord walked to our table carrying a frothy mug of hot chocolate. "Good morning fellow traveler," he said, and swiped up the check with blue numbers added up on back side. "On me," he said.

"Thank you," O.W. said. His voice was low and expressionless. He was trying. Mama was right.

"Well take your time. We'll stretch our legs."

Little Cedric walked up, joined his father. They'd left the woman whose bright lips had faded overnight at their booth, which had no phone on it, I noticed.

"Have you two met?" Big Cedric asked.

He shook his head, the boy who was a miniature of his father, the same soft flab under his chin and china blue eyes. Their hands, both of them, were long-fingered and clean, the nails done, even on the boy. Prominent noses, though I'd never had thought that then, how it was a mark of good blood, a prominent schnaz.

"Cedric, Joey. Joey, Cedric."

We shook. The food was getting cold. Some of the other drivers had big black boots propped out from under their tables, were smoking, talking into phones. The driver's bathrooms had showers in them, and there was a naked man wiping off on a towel when I brushed my teeth. He smiled at me, winked.

"Morning little cowpoke," he said.

Back outside, the company was loaded. Mr. Lord said everyone's names into the microphone, and Cedric got to sing, "*On top of spaghetti, all covered with cheese, I lost my poor meatball, when somebody sneezed.*"

There were sixteen of us, eighteen counting me and Captain Harvell, who'd chauffeured us through the night *marvelously*, Lord said, his voice a little thick from the champagne mimosa station mid-bus. By New Jersey, they'd all got soused all over again, a steady stream grinning at me in line for the john.

One lady handed me a piece of chocolate, lifted a finger to her lips, said, "*shhh,*" just when the door sign went vacant.

I said, "shhh," our secret.

There are moments when your life changes right before your eyes. I've seen it happen four times at least, when the here and now gets this shine to it, sometimes for the good, sometimes not, sometimes both at the same time, and you know that the very next instant you will shed for all time the you you've been, and be this person you've been moving toward your whole life. It happened the first time I heard the voice over the phone of the woman who'd be my wife, how it went through me like a jolt from an electric fence and I knew that it was the voice I'd been listening for since before I could remember. When the silver dollar of my daughter's head shone during birth, and I'd counted *one, two, three, push* with her mother's hand in mine, I saw it coming, a me who'd no longer think *me, me, me, I, I, I*, but *you, us*, and that has made all the difference. The photograph from our thirtieth anniversary trip, with Notre Dame and the Seine behind our backs, the wind crazy in our hair, it caught that moment when I for the first time understood that we'd make it, Renee and I. And that dizzy minute in 1972 when we rolled up in front of the Waldorf Astoria, the name in gold above three stone towered turrets, a white-gloved steward in a tuxedo and tails saluting us there with the lit up wreathes behind his back, and the yellow cabs honk-honking with flags aflutter on either side of the three-doored entrance, blue sky and the smell of city. I gazed out the window through the doors at a hundred yards of marble floor flowing under one chandelier to the next, and knew in a heartbeat that Mama'd been right to send me here, and that I was now turned in a direction that none of us could have fathomed or foreseen.

Three uniformed bellmen joined O.W. at the bus's under compartment, their muscles bulging as they hauled out the oversized Arky suitcases loaded six days to Sunday for the theater and Sunday Brunch in Peacock Alley, for Tiffany's and the guided tour to the top of the Empire State Building, for the Italian Feast to be had after *Grease*, which had in its score the music Mama'd grown up dancing to, she'd told me, sock hops and doo-wop, big-finned music with all the chrome. Those suitcases were heavy and they filled a whole lot of wheeled gurneys that disappeared through the triple doors where I caught a whiff of fresh cut flowers and what I did not know was jazz from a trio inside. The chief of the bellmen held the door open with his white-gloved hand for all the passersby of our party, the last of which was Cedric Lord, junior then senior, walking toward a huge Christmas tree with a trainload of wrapped and ribboned gifts I just caught sight of before the door shut, and it was just me and O.W. and a hundred honking taxis as far as the eye could see, the wind whistling through the U.S. flag and another that was green, red and white— Italian, I'd learn, pesto, sauce, and pasta.

"We're not staying?" I said, words O.W. no doubt gauged and fully registered then and thereafter. It'd been a long haul, about half of which he'd driven illegally. Eight hours on, eight off, I didn't know the rules then.

"We're not far. All aboard."

And in the microphone as he drove away from the Waldorf and the Lord party, he announced the landmarks and sights as we passed. "Over there is Broadway. Keep an eye out for Madison Square Garden." He pointed out Rockefeller Center and Yankee Stadium, the team he'd actually been drafted by to play outfield for, only he wanted to pitch and turned them down. It was a true story, I'd one day find out. He could have played in the majors, O.W.

I was of course lost by the time we got where we were going, parked the bus, and carried what I remember now was not a suitcase but a paper bag with my church donated clothes inside. Our room was tiny, the size of our bathroom back home, one bed you pulled down from the wall, but there was a window, and a whole lot of traffic outside, miles of concrete to the Hudson Bay where we'd see the Statue of Liberty in a day or two, O.W. said, unpacking underwear and socks into the chest of drawers, hanging the extra driver's shirt in the tiny closet. Then he pulled down the bed, took off his coat and Trailways tie, the shiny black boots, lay down and went still as stone, while I watched the rabbit-eared TV shows and people and voices foreign as the man from the moon.

Sometime late, I woke, the traffic still hells bells outside, this white fuzz and static on the television that I've since learned is fossil radiation from the Big Bang.

I was to be included in all tours, Mama's doing. I wouldn't learn till too late that O.W.'d given me his slot, his ticket to the Broadway show and seat at the feast to follow. He had a food stipend from Trailways of ten bucks a day, and we blew through the whole thing for breakfast at a diner across from the hotel, biscuits and gravy for both of us, buttery eggs and home fries, toast on the side. Then he hailed a cab, told the driver Waldorf Astoria.

I said, "Aren't you coming, Daddy?"

It was the first time he'd been out of his bus driver uniform, so it looked like him again, instead of Captain Harvell. "Nope," he said. "I got plenty to do."

"How do I get back?"

He said, "Here," handed me a five-dollar bill wrapped around a hotel card with the name and address of where we were staying. "Do what I just did, and give'em that."

He shut the door, walked off. I didn't have a key. How would I get in? When would I be home? That's what I was thinking when the driver blasted off into the traffic—he was a maniac, honk-honking and speeding and passing, flipping the bird and cussing in a language I didn't understand, then smiling at me in the rearview. It was my first time ever in a taxicab and it scared the shit out of me, so when the Waldorf bellhop opened the door to let me inside the screamingly opulent lobby, the first thing I asked was *where is the men's room?* The black man gave me the biggest of smiles, said, "Here, follow me, chief." He walked me past a big glittering clock with strange numbers made of letters, Xs and Vs, held the door open for me and pointed. Inside sat two toilets, side by side, a riddle for the ages.

Overnight, there'd been a sighting of Ann Margaret and Warren Beatty, so our whole party was in a tizzy, gathered in a corridor of lobby called Peacock Alley from whence issued jazz and the aroma of all good things to eat. Both Cedrics were there, the marvelous red-lipped woman in a black dress and heels, the confidant who'd slipped me chocolate and her grey-bearded husband, the rest, everyone dressed up like they were going to a wedding or church, the way people from the sticks will every time because they've never known the privilege of casual arrogance, not even for their money.

Little Cedric had blue eyes. He saw me before I saw him, his father reading off rules and relations from the notebook he ever carried, scribbling this and that—in all my life the only thing I'd ever seen O.W. write down was his log book entries, which were mostly forged.

"How was your night?" little Cedric said.

I said, "They have different TV stations here."

He whistled—a soft high note. "I talked to my mother. Out room is a suite. It has a spare bed. Maybe you can stay with us."

The sound and smell and feel of hard tile beneath my feet, all the voices and chandelier lights reflecting off mirrored walls, it made me dizzy, but in a good way, I think. O.W. was back up in that room snoring on the pull down bed, how strange it was, sharing his space.

"Everybody gather together," big Cedric said. "This is Fernando. He will be our guide today. Fernando?"

He was a college student, Fernando, the first one I'd ever met. He carried a red flag with a lion on it for Spain, where he was from, before he came here to study history at Columbia. We were to stay close enough to see the red flag at all times. If we got lost, stay still, he'd return for us. We must have on walking shoes, wear a coat because a storm was forecast to move in from the Atlantic. We were not to give anything to strangers nor to take their pictures without asking. There would be lunch at Katz's Deli and vespers if we wanted at St. Patrick's Cathedral. Was anyone afraid of heights? Faint of heart? Questions?

"Will there be time for shopping?"

The red-lipped woman in her black dress and heels looked like a movie star, and I was glad that she was one of us, one of our party. Her name was Lisa, and she was somehow related to the Stephens family who owned half of Arkansas, timber and soy and bauxite. She was screwing big Cedric in the upstairs suite.

Little Cedric rolled his eyes. "Lisa-pisa," he said.

Fernando waived his red flag. "Of course," he said. "Times Square. The center of the universe."

Lisa Stephens squealed. "Goody," she said.

Fernando formed us into a line, and we followed him two-by-two into the day where a stiff wind blew down the street corridor. Whirling around me then, the whole decadent world. Sight, smell, sound and taste, the city shuddered up through the soles of my feet. The day blurred. A red flag with lions flapping on the roof of the Empire State Building, softball beneath leafless trees in Central Park. Nuts cooked over embers, the street vendors scooped them salty into cones, and the taste of exhaust got under my teeth. There was a subway and winos passed out on a floor that stuck to your shoes, tokens cold between the fingers, I tasted pastrami for the first time, and the mustard had seeds that stuck between the teeth. Radio City's Rockettes lifted naked legs, and the ice skates glittered like fire. Someone said they'd never seen so many dressed up Arkies in their life, or was that me? something I said years later?

We followed Fernando through thick and thin and when it started snowing, these big magical flakes that fell down through the bright lights and laughter and languages foreign as thunder, we arrived back where we had started, me and little Cedric, Lisa-pisa and Lord.

"You're more like us than him," Cedric said. "Ask if you can stay over."

I'd unrolled the five-dollar bill, and was about to walk outside to hail my first cab, a thought that had my heart beating despite the daylong tour of Manhattan.

"Promise," he said

It was Friday night, December 22nd, 1972, snowing in New York City. A bevy of elves carried a silver gurney lined in cedar branches where lay a suckling pig with a yellow apple in its mouth. Music rained down from on high.

I said, "I promise," waved O.W.'s five in the air, so the wind took it, and I had to sprint into the street and stomp it underfoot.

Of late, O.W.'s appeared in my dream life. In his eighties, with his great grandmother's long-lived blood, he's young again in my dream, we're walking from a hotel, many of us walking with Daddy at just daylight. There's been a drama behind us, but I've forgotten that—in the new light. He's in his Trailways suit, Daddy, and I'm in front, to his right. A street turns away from our path, and I start that way, only it's a dead-end, no place to park a bus, and I realize he's down around the bend in a field—a school playground?—and I see it there, our bus. It dawns on me, walking that way, that it's fall, and the street is ankle deep with the most exquisite good-smelling leaves, how they crunch underfoot. An acorn shines, big as a golf ball, a green sheen, disappears, then I find three more, gather them because I know that my daughter will want to see these, that she is like me in the heart about this moment when I am both father and son. The passengers walk by, and Daddy, the bus just up there. A yellow pear glows from branches cut in a trash bin—I pick it, breath the aroma, on the road, this will be good to eat. And I think that this walk through the deep leaves in low light to the bus is the finest moment of my life, surely a time to remember, that anyone who has ever loved me would love. That's what I'm thinking in my dream, ankle-deep in leaves, the bright shining acorns. I think to remember, the leaves, the golden light.

All these years I've blocked this out for the other, the grimier story, the one where our power's always turned off and we've torn down the neighbor's wood fence to cook pinto beans, and Mama's always depressed and Daddy's either a mean drunk or off in Florida getting sober, but there was a world before that, between the brawls and beatings and the world I inhabited as a teen. The one where Daddy wore his crisp Trailways suit and sharp-billed hat, when he'd driven a charter bus for rich people out of Little Rock, up the coast to New York City with twelve-year-old me, on the cusp, how that must have been, how it must have looked through my eyes.

There were grapes in the eye sockets of the suckling pig, the ones the elves whistled through the Waldorf's triple doors. A bed of romaine underneath it, circled with white asparagus, the rarest of all, and cherries, festive, three days before Christmas. This was the trip that would cost him his job—we'd end up working at a truck stop gas station he'd buy and lose in desperation. There'd be a pool hall with a secret bedroom out back, a jukebox that played the Eagles—"Tequila Sunrise," "Take it Easy," "The Last Resort." I'd learn to change tires, patch and puncture-stop flats on the machine, pump supreme, the little bells dinging. I'd make my vow to get the hell out of Dodge, and stick to my guns. And it all started, maybe it did, that snowy afternoon when Little Cedric said that I was more like him than O.W.

Maybe I was.

The play was *Grease*.

Of course it was. In a theater bigger than First Baptist, the Methodist and Church of Christ put together times four. Mirrors and bright lights ambushed you at every turn, and women in high heels and Santa hats drank wine from fluted glasses in front of a giant painting of a grizzly bear fighting a bull bloodied by a stream of red and purple flowers sewn into its spine. Everyone was talking their fast New York talk, even the Arkies had sped up their tongues as we entered the throng on Saturday night before Sunday Christmas, and there were men in the bathroom dressed in tuxedos with Christmassy bow ties and cummerbunds. White gloved attendants carried warm towels for you to wipe your hands on after you peed into stand-up urinals that reflected the eyes I'd inherited from the father I'd never met out in Arizona, my grandfather's hawk nose and brown hair, thick and unruly with a little dandruff sifting down my shoulders. Probably the clip-on tie was a crooked, but clean. Seeing my face reflected in the Broadway urinal before curtain call, *Grease* about to fly down the pike, the whole big spinning world and all that I did not know was hidden from my twelve years as the dark carp swimming beneath the frozen pond when I rode Shawnee onto the ice and cracks zinged away in each of the seven directions. Should that person see this one, the one I've become, what might he think? Would he recognize me as kin? Would he think himself better than me? And I him?

Bits of memory flash, the moment the curtains stirred, real live people playing music from the pit, and voices rose up from the darkened stage where a spotlight fell on three Pink Ladies. Their skin showed. They smacked gum. A fourth one had met a boy in summer at the beach, they'd fallen in love, they'd had a blast.

The row of us sat on the main floor, stage left, I was near the far aisle. Everyone had disappeared. There was a sadness in the song, a longing I did not know, but would. I'd feel it in my heart the summer before senior year, when me and Danny Layne drove up to Greer's Ferry and when it got dark we all walked down to the boat ramp in our swimsuits. We met these girls who smelled like oranges beneath a field of stars, and somebody drove their car down and put a Peter Frampton eight-track in, and the song was "Lines on My Face," with its long drawn out melodic lead up front drifting over the still water reflecting stars and the fireworks popping off across the lake, so I knew for the first time that a season of my life had passed—I'd never get it back, and that was sad and okay.

They were eighteen, the character, these boys with slicked back hair who sang *shuda bop bop*, you whisper in my ear, *shuda bob bob de wop*, and I thought of Mama and O.W., how it must have been for them, to be young and in love, the sock hops and doo-wop, the big-finned life and living.

Vince Fontain, the Main Brain, the Vel-doo-Rays, *baby baby how I want you*, the girls smoked cigarettes in the next scene, in bed, and one pierced the other's ear. The boys, who were called T Birds sang *Go Greased Lightning* so it sounded like Elvis and Conway Twitty and Jerry Lee all rolled up into one, I could see their eyes, the actors', and they could see mine. I thought so, it seemed that way. If I could just have a car, a Camaro with a T-top—automatic, systematic, hydrometric—Greased Lightning.

One boy pulled his pants down so you could see his full white ass. He sang the praise and magic of mooning: *a wop bop a loo bob a wop bam boom.*

Sixth grade, we'd had our first dance, though it was kind of put offish, all the big tall girls standing on one side of the gym, boys on the other, these long-haired hippies playing "Smoke on the Water," and after we played spin the bottle and I had to kiss Natalie Pierce, who tasted like Juicy Fruit and Tang. On stage they danced the hand jive, sang *baby, baby*, the boys and the girls, the dance moves whirling and outrageous, and the curtain closed.

I forget just about everything after intermission. My wife's Aunt Pat used to suffer dry drunk, where she'd be cowboy-plowed, only she hadn't had a thing. That's what I had for the rest of my first night on Broadway. On stage, one of the girls had got pregnant, and I was old enough to know how that happened, but not that it would happen to me and a deacon's daughter nor what we'd do after. One of the girls was a beauty school dropout, and that made me think of Mama, I guess because she worked at Maybelline, came home after stuffing lipstick molds all day long, washed her hands in the sink that was forever stained Aristotle Red or Burnt Sienna.

It was a false alarm, the pregnant girl. The good girl went bad, said *the hell with it*, dressed in tight leather and I swear to God I still smell her sweet sticky horniness from the aisle seats through the walls of time. There was dinner after, Italian, men carrying huge platters, and one crashed on the floor. Before I knew it I was swept back to the fold-out where O.W. snored and moaned and sometimes stopped breathing.

Snow was falling.

It fell through the neon diner sign across the street, blew up the sidewalk where a man with a blanket over his shoulders leaned against the wall, blowing a silver horn into the sky.

Sunday morning, Christmas Eve, 1972, O.W. dressed in the pressed pants and black boots, the fresh shirt, put on the hat with its shiny black bill, and I followed him down the maze of streets to where the Trailways Charter was parked, where we cleaned up a mess of beer bottles and schnapps that had mysteriously been drunk and scattered during our stay. The glass clinked into a cardboard box he'd found outside, and our eyes met a few times during the cleaning. Tomorrow was Christmas. Today we were on our way to Niagara Falls, then on to Detroit, where a dinner was planned in this tower that overlooked the Motor City, what Lord called it. O.W. and I were invited—we had seats at the table, and a menu had gone around with three choices for entree: *Gigot d'Agneau Rôti* (Roast Leg of Lamb), *Filets de Poisson Gratinés, á la Parisenne* (Fish Filets Poached in White wine with Cream and Egg Yolk Sauce), and *Poulet Poele a L'Estragon Farce Duxelles* (Casserole-roasted Chicken with Taragon and Mushroom Stuffing). Cheesecake was dessert, which I thought odd—the only cheese we ever had at our house was Velveeta, and I could not for the life of me imagine a cake made of it, though I was game. To tell the truth, if the rich folk were eating shit on a stick, I'd of taken mine and given it a try, after a night of soaring theater, the bright lights and big city had got into my blood.

"How was your show?" O.W. asked on the way to the Waldorf. We passed a cathedral where these deep bells rang out one, two, three, nine times. The snow had stopped and the sun was out, sort of, in between skyscrapers were pools of light and warmth. People were walking their dogs on short leashes.

"It was good," I said. "Mama'd like it."

The bus had been washed, vacuumed, only it smelled like beer. Big Cedric wouldn't like it, nor the red-lipped woman who I saw stand up and shake it during "Greased Lightning." Maybe there was a hint of cigarette smoke, too, someone had lit up on the bus. I thought about the bathroom behind my seat, the little bowl full of blue water.

"What about me?" His eyes were blue in the rearview, the little white scar on his cheek where Mama'd got him with a fingernail. "You think I'd like it."

I said, "Did you drink on the bus? And smoke?"

I was hungry. We'd skipped breakfast, and now just sat out there waiting, me and O.W., for our party to walk through the glass doors. There was a long haul in front of us, to Niagara and Detroit, the revolving restaurant tower.

O.W. said, "You and your fancy friends."

And their they were, followed by a silver gurney loaded with suitcases that were even heavier now after Christmas shopping and chocolate shops and cognac, t-shirts and little plastic snow globes with the empire state building inside.

The white-gloved bellman waved when we pulled away, and there was O.W. in the bright wedge of mirror. His father had been a driver just like him, East Texas Motor Freight. The old man had helped him get hired to work the docks straight out of high school. For a while he was a chauffeur in the Army, driving generals into secret tunnels outside DC in Virginia where the underground second government was housed. His people, they lived on Thayer in Little Rock, working class, the one girl, Aunt Judy, hell bent on getting out. She'd run away with a Polish electrician who built her a house in Baltimore, and she swore she'd never come home unless somebody died. Which of course they did, and did again, so by the time she met me in New York, New York outside DC to tell how Jimmy'd died in a one car crash, we'd stood together grave to grave.

Fancy friends.

He'd say it to me, O.W., while kicking me out of the house one day, referring to a professor from the University who'd written a movie script that he'd had to shake hands with when I won those prizes. He was kicking me out of the house for coming home with beer on my breath—*why don't you go live with your fancy friends*, he'd say. Some days when he was home from his run, he'd sit at the kitchen table and clean his pistol.

"What you going to do, O.W? Shoot me?"

"I don't need a gun for you," he'd say. "Get out."

And that's what I did, got out. I'd end up in Mobile, Alabama, at a bus station, calling Mom Dee collect, promising to pay her back. She'd drive me to Fayetteville where I'd get on with a roofer the first day, then a framing crew that bricklayers hired me away from, so I'd be able to rent the Hill Street house where I'd meet Renee on Easter Sunday, fall in love and move to DC. Jimmy'd die in a car wreck on May 9, and one year later—to the exact day—I'd graduate from University the day before Mother's Day. I'd give Mama my mortar board and tassel, she'd be bloated with lupus, and they'd drive four hours home to Lonoke, stop through Solgahatchia on the way, where Jimmy was buried in the family cemetery on the authentic Trail of Tears. I'd picture her there on her knees beside his grave, praying and crying and screaming *why oh why, Lord,* on my graduation day, first one in our family ever. We'd move to Carolina, me and Renee, marry, Utah not on our radar yet, but not so far away. I'd never go home again. I think about it sometimes when me and my daughter argue, and sometimes I say the thing that crosses the line. That moment had been the last straw between us, me and O.W.—*your fancy friends*

What I remember about Niagara Falls: it was a big ass waterfall, and way back when folks had ridden over the top in barrels and tight rope walkers stretched ropes one side to the other and tiptoed over, framed by the rainbows that hovered in between, our guide said. Newlyweds travel there to be photographed while embracing and French kissing, and once one had got cold feet and pushed the other off. The son of a bitch had frozen bottom to top, 167 feet, one winter and ice climbers climbed it with picks and pancake spikes. I remember mist on my face and the white water sound I'd learn later in life, when we'd scout rapids that had taken lives so their personalities had grown and you could hear them growl—some of them like Lava, which could rip an eighteen foot raft to pieces, take you under to where the light disappeared and hold you there till kingdom come—and you'd feel the cold mist on your face, it was like that, the lot of us Arkies freezing our asses off, a rainbow between us and Canada. I remember being glad I wasn't riding down in a barrel, that I didn't have to tightrope the yawning mouth, the sound of it, the mist on my face. I wanted to show Mama, to take the photograph from their honeymoon and frame it in silver, the rainbow behind them, her and O.W., another country at their backs with its clean slate—tomorrow was Christmas, anything at all could happen.

From the back of the bus as we drove away and the lunch meats and cheeses were coming out and big Cedric had quit bitching about how our bus smelt like a brewery, when the mimosas were mixed and long-neck Budweisers cracked—what on earth had happened to the imports, the Heineken and Corona?—I watched the rainbow recede and thought about how close I'd come to another country, where they used different money and spoke another language.

Little Cedric asked if he could sit with me. "Pisa's such a bitch," he said, and we made our smoked turkey sandwiches, a paper plate full of Lay's chips for each of us. He hustled back two frosty root beers and we snorked.

On the microphone, Big Cedric explained about our dinner that night, how he'd heard you could see Santa and his reindeer from up in the revolving tower, and maybe everyone who wasn't naughty would receive a gift. Mr. Lord regarded O.W., wagged an index finger and shook his head. Then he launched into "Here Comes Santa Clause," in his fake Elvis voice—*he sees you when you're sleeping, he knows when you're awake.*

Little Cedric put his fingers in his ears.

We flew toward Detroit, O.W. up there beyond the red-lipped lady, eyes like chunks of ice. I thought of Mama and Jimmy and Christmas Eve at Mom Dee's, how we all got to open a gift, and once Uncle Earl had driven us all to his barn in a snowstorm—because that's what his gift had said to do, a little note with blue writing inside a box that said drive to the barn. The headlights shone into the corral, these silver dollar flakes whirling, and there reared a Palomino stallion his wife had written a hot check for, and he leapt up on the horse's back, and it bucked him off, and he got up bloody-lipped in the headlight glow, everyone's eyes glowing demon red.

They named it Comanche, the palomino. After our house burned and we moved into the back of Uncle's pasture, I'd see him glowing out under a full moon, the pale mane and tail streaming. The horse had died mysteriously, and Uncle Earl collected insurance money, a thin white scar where he'd split his lip that Christmas eve with the headlights crazy on the rodeo Santa perpetrated by a felony hot check.

Mama, everybody, always looked away from Uncle's transgressions—he was family. No one talked about his jail time. Family forgives. Maybe crazy families like us forgive most of all.

We called Mama before dressing for dinner. This time around we got a hotel room with the rest of our party, so the room was nice with a phone whose red light blinked when it rang and a bathroom with a whole stack of bright white towels and little soaps in plastic packages, shampoos and body lotions. Somebody'd folded the tag end of the toilet paper into a triangle point. Imagine that, somebody's job in that Detroit 3 Star hotel was to fold people's toilet paper into a triangle, so that just before you wiped your butt, you could do the math, flash back to the time you first hear that *hypotenuse* is the side of the triangle that is opposite the right angle.

"Merry Christmas," she said when she answered the phone. "Hello?"

I said, "Mama."

Arkansas was south and an hour earlier, so it was still afternoon, not dark like Detroit. Our phone back home was a party line, neighbors, who knows who, always picking up, listening in—you could hear them breathe.

"How are you Joe? How did you like New York? Tell me about your play." O.W. was tying his tie in the bathroom mirror, all lit up and shining. He held one finger up in the mirror, which I guessed meant I had one minute—it was long distance, we'd called collect.

I said, "Good, Mama." And I wanted to tell her about the moment we rolled up to the Waldorf, and the bellman in white gloves, how corned beef pastrami tasted with spicy mustard on rye, how the man in the bathroom dried your hands for you, about the red-lipped woman and how little Cedric had proclaimed me better than O.W. Maybe one day I'd be able to make it clear for her how it had felt to be there in front of the stage where boys in black leather sang "Greased Lightning" just like Elvis, who she'd once touched, when he came to Little Rock, not yet famous, but close. He'd looked her in the eye, Mama claimed, and she knew he'd send his man to bring her back stage, and that she'd go, and that at sweet sixteen her life would get up and go, that she'd fall for an Air Force boy and elope to Tucson and birth me in the desert at Christmas time, then fly away home on a Greyhound bus, so I'd never know about any of it until it was too late to matter. I couldn't tell her that then because I didn't know, not yet. But I could feel it in my gut, that I was somehow different. Not better, just different.

"You'd love it," I said.

"How's Daddy?" I could hear it in the background, her record player, Elvis singing "Blue Christmas."

I said, "We're going to dinner tonight in the tower. There's fish, chicken or lamb."

The knot tight beneath his Adam's apple, O.W. motioned for the phone. "Here," he said.

I said, "Love you, got to go."

Low and deep, he told her that we'd be driving home tomorrow, Christmas Day, because the roads would be mostly clear, people would be with their families, and we were between storms. "Don't look for us before midnight," he said. "I love you."

After, I clipped on my tie and we joined our party in the first floor lobby. Five cabs ferried us to the foot of the tower for our final meal together. The elevator to the top took forever.

The details of that fancy dinner blur, though I remember that each chair had a white setting in front of it, a starched napkin folded into a *fleur de lis*, and on top of the smallest plate was a card imprinted with the name of who was supposed to sit there, and they'd misspelled our last names, me and O.W. We sat facing each other on either side of the end farthest from big and little Cedric, Lisa Stephens, and the rest of them whose faces have blended together over the years. I wouldn't know them now if they walked up and bit me on the butt, that's how O.W.'d put it, *stupid as a sackful of hammers, shit out of luck, pie aren't square, pie are round, come back and bite you on the butt,* the bits and phrases I've now passed to my own progeny.

There was a view, and the sudden nausea when you realized how high up you were. The men were all ordering high balls—water will be fine me and daddy said, though our places were set with two wine glasses apiece, three forks, two spoons and a knife—no salt nor pepper on the table, which I'd later learn meant high class, because only poor white trash salted and peppered their food at the table, that was the hired help's job, and if they got it wrong, fire they asses. Cedric made a toast to the party, to the day, to 1973, the New Year at hand, may it be a good one for us all. Lake Erie sprawled out beyond the city lights, cold water I imagined, like Ouachita outside Hot Springs where Mama's daddy was fishing guide at Shangri La Boat Dock. Cedric toasted everything you could shake a stick at, told a naughty joke so his mistress laughed so hard that red wine came out her nose, and she had to sop it up with the starched white napkin from her lap. Finally, he got to Daddy. He held his shining bourbon and ginger with a squeeze of lemon up before us and said he'd like to offer a toast to our magnificent driver, who'd brought us through thick and thin and who could blame such a man if he reached into the cookie jar a time or two.

Here's to Captain Harvell," Mr. Lord said. "*Salud.*"

Someone knocked a fork on an empty glass, the ding, ding, ding, somehow taking the lights down, some, just a little, and I could see Little Cedric looking at me from the other end, in his chair beside Lisa Stephen who was screwing his father, while his mother was at home minding the brother and sisters.

"Here, here," big Cedric said, and the food and drink descended on us all at once from every direction: hot rolls with whipped butter, little bowls with olives and cheeses and fish eggs. A man who moved so fast you couldn't see him fill the glasses with red and white wine, and I could smell the bouquet of each and thought that I might like it, the wine, quite rightly as it turned out—nothing like the unsweetened Welch's grape juice in the tiny shot glasses passed around with bits of bitter cracker for the Lord's Supper on Easter Sunday when we'd sing UP FROM THE GROUND HE AROSE, and Yvonne Spence would gaze down at me from the choir loft, and it would all mix together, the wine and the smokey eyed woman and bitter bread, how the church had gone Amen-crazy, *hallelujah, hallelujah* that day when O.W.'d walked down the aisle, as if Satan's right hand man had flipped to the Lord, and the world would be a better place from there on out. Baptists were, of course, forbidden to drink wine, which was of course why there was never a single place to park out at county line liquor, burned down, rebuilt, burned down and rebuilt again, big as a barn.

"*Poisson, Poulet*, or the *Gigot* for the gentleman?" the waiter who was too fast to see was asking us. Caesar salads had appeared on clear glass plates, and the lady who'd slipped me a chocolate had squealed when she bit into a lacy fish skeleton hidden under a crouton. O.W. said, "Lamb."

"Of course. *Et tu?*"

I said, "*Brute*," and the waiter was suddenly visible. He smiled down at me, nodded. "I see they teach Shakespeare down in Dixie where literary composition is clearly esteemed. Try the fish. Tonight's the night for the feast of seven fishes, you know."

"The fish," I said.

"*Poisson. Tres bien. Et tu, Brute*," he said and laughed from down deep.

O.W. was looking at me over the full glasses of Cabernet and white. He had a way of turning his head to the side so you could tell he was thinking, like when I told him I was going to college. Jimmy'd follow, for a year, two. O.W. blamed my brother's stutter on the academy, bunch of snooty know-goddamn-know-it-alls.

We ate our salads surrounded by chatter—I'd not learned to talk and eat at the same time, still have trouble with it, so our table at home was mostly quiet, save the prayer, and the tinkling light fixture when planes flew over.

The tower restaurant revolved—we were traveling in circles, facing without even knowing it the seven holy directions I'd one day learn from the Mandan woman who'd one day sing my death song: in front, behind, on either side, above, below, and inside—the seventh direction. It was a real deal feast, the whole nine yards, eating high on the hog, shitting in high cotton, all that and more. But mostly it felt like just me and O.W., him giving me that sideways look like I'd said he descended from an ape, a shit-eating *go-rilla*, me and my fancy friends, dumb ass bus driver.

My betrayal? Having read *Julius Caesar. Et tu, Brute*? That's how it felt that Christmas when I was twelve, riding circles in the revolving tower.

The entrees arrived, the fast waiter ground pepper from a grinder long as my leg. "Enough?" he said.

"Enough," O.W. said.

"And for little Shakespeare?"

"Enough," I said before he ground a flake.

"Enjoy. Save room for cheesecake."

We ate in silence, face to face. Neither of us touched the wine. The bread was cold, the whipped butter. The fish and the lamb, both Christian symbols for Christ the Savior, born of a virgin in a barn where donkeys brayed, on this very night when it was said that animals talked. My birth had been a troublesome one. Mom Dee had driven out to Tucson, as had her ex-husband, my grandfather Si, with his new wife, Ruby. O.W. was nowhere on the map. My blood father was in jail. It was Christmas Eve, just like tonight, and the doc would walk out and say the mother won't make it, or the boy won't make it, or I'm sorry but it looks like we can't save either. And they'd prayed in the waiting room, even Si, old warlock that he was.

In Tucson, where it had been a wet year, and snow glowed Christmas morning up on Mount Lemon. And of course we both made it. Mama fled Tucson for Arkansas, but the blood father got out of jail, tracked us, attempted kidnap. Mama found O.W., she was his second wife, and no one fucked with them. He'd adopted me, only they'd missed the final legal procedure, and it was never legally formalized that I was O.W.'s son, that my last name was his—I never found out till after Mama died when we were traveling to Spain and I ran into a roadblock at the passport agency. It could have gone either way. My wedding license was in limbo, my daughter's name. My degrees. The house title. Everything.

I petitioned courts in both states, paid the fees and made it legal. And I've never said a word of this to O.W., that I chose to be his son, and not the other way around.

His rack of lamb was rare—it leaked red blood all over the white plate, but he was good with the knife, separated the three ribs, sopped blood with a buttered roll.

"It's good," he said, looked at me and nodded.

"The fish, too," I said.

"Good."

The next morning, my thirteenth birthday which we'd decided not to tell any of our party about because it might take away something of their own Christmas, we headed south, left the Great Lakes behind us. Ohio on one side, Indiana on the other. In front of us, Kentucky and then Tennessee. We'd re-cross Mississippi River into Arkansas, and someone up front yelled *whoo pig sooie* over the loudspeaker. Drive right on past the exit sign for Lonoke and home where Mama and Jimmy lay sleeping. It was dark, the sky starless. We barreled down Highway 40 past the Remington plant, and Maybelline, headed for a new year, a clean slate, the chance to start all over again.

I think of O.W. at the helm of the Trailways bus, in his uniform, the captain's hat, clean shaven, his face alight in the four-foot rearview. Blue eyed ice cubes gazing before and after. He'd never missed a turn, not yet. For a while he'd chosen the right course. He had. Above, below, on either side, up, down, we navigated the night by the sheer instinct of his unknowable heart.

Burning Down My Father's House

I once thought to burn down my father's house. It happens like this: I've flown into Little Rock though everyone thinks I'm floating the Green as I often do, four days rafting from Flaming Gorge to Swallow Canyon, slaying calf-length browns on golden rapalas. I don't seem to notice that my flight is traceable to my name, or even if I rent a car and drive my credit cards will light up my tracks. Truth is, it's hard to burn down your father's house without getting caught. However I get there, I get there, and I've rented a car, and brought one of those 2.5 gallon red plastic gas cans like the one at home that has MOWER written on it in permanent black marker. I've filled it to the brim, the gas can, and you can smell where it spilled in the back floorboard, hear it slosh at the J-Ville exit where I hang a Louie toward Foxgrave Country Club where Daddy's house is built off the front nine, and leaning against the garage is the hot tub Mama drowned in, his trophy.

It's always late afternoon, when I break in, the refrigerator contents showing he hadn't changed a bit, same six-month old Styrofoam tray of brown hamburger meat, fetid pasta, light beer, some bacon and a slice of country club cake in plastic from Foxgrave just down the way.

That's not fair—Mama's the one who let the hamburger go bad.

I smell him.

The musk from when him and Mama shared the same closet, his shirts and underwear down by the shoes, the green road suitcase from whence Mama once pulled a condom and baked it into the Sunday meatloaf, made sure he got the right piece. I'd watched him put it into his mouth and make the discovery, look at Mama across the table, blue eyes hard as pond ice.

He hadn't come from country club people.

His daddy drove for ETW and C, and was a local driver who masked the whiskey on his breath with Certs, which he always kept in the front pocket of the Pendleton shirt he wore in winter, a white wife beater in summer. I'd stayed with him and Evelyn the August Mama birthed Jimmy, and I'd missed her, silly six-year-old me, and had picked a bouquet of red tulips from his front yard for her, and he'd spanked my ass with a belt—for picking flowers.

Evelyn, his mother, she was a crazy drunk who'd offer you a pickle to kiss her, then she'd go in the bedroom and try to kill herself, so Daddy's brother Chester'd have to drive her to the ER, and they'd sew her up or pump her stomach and she'd be home again, there on Thayer, across the street from a paraplegic who'd lay in the deep grass of his front yard, face up, so you could see his teeth. Daddy and Uncle Chester'd played baseball with his son, they'd talk to him and he'd recognize their voices, call each by name, tell a dirty joke.

Some Black Panthers had moved in up the street so O.W. Senior kept a single barrel shotgun leaned in every corner. I stayed there some nights—where they mixed and drank their whiskey I have no idea, I never witnessed a single bottle, not ever, but it was always on their breath, always.

They never got fall down drunk, never passed or black out. I could just sense a difference, a glint in their eyes, hot brown like Chester, who'd go on to pitch for the St. Louis Cardinals—go ahead, run his name, my daughter and I have, his ERA and win-loss record. Daddy'd played with Brooks Robinson, got his autograph for me at the Central High 40th where he and Mama'd attended a get together of the Tigers and Doughboys. *Dear Joe,* it says, *could your old man ever rock and fire.* And I guess he could, all those afternoon pitch out sessions on the new cut grass that stained the white cleats he'd bought me for Pony League. *Rock and fire,* he'd say, bang a fist into the mitt.

I've never actually *seen* the house I've come to burn down. So I haven't really processed key points like where to park or registered who's home and might eyewitness me amongst these neighbors, country club snoots who lay out at the pool then practice their pitching wedges on the practice green, Ping putter in one gloved hand, wedge in the other. And I'm the sort of person that makes people suspicious, always have been. Cop sees me driving down the road, on come the lights. And even once, when I'd showed up at the Utah Supreme Court because the Chief Justice, Don Dierling who was a friend of mine, who was giving me the pick of his personal library before retiring, his wife Nina was late to meet me at the courthouse door and I'd stood inside the rotunda till the security guard got a look at me, and stood their glaring for a solid minute until I couldn't take any more and walked outside. There came Nina walking up, so I told her—about the security guard who'd glared, how I'd never been one time to court for a good reason. "You're such a strange man, Joe," she'd said, and I guess it was true—regular folk could smell it on my breath, the strangeness.

It was, of course, imperative that O.W. not see me. He was a smart motherfucker and without surprise on my side, I didn't stand a chance. I was toast if he saw me first, and he'd know exactly why I'd come, had been waiting for a long time for me to do so, probably wondering where the hell I was, what was taking me so long—why did I have to be such a woodpussy? Once I had some girls over and yes we had some liquor—small potatoes, peppermint schnapps, maybe, or Wellers. And I'd called IceLand to ask for his ETA, when would he be home? And he'd called the house straight away from the mobile in his long white International, said, "You're not having a party in my house. Send the floozies home. And you'd best take your booze back where you got it from." Just like that. I didn't say a word, sent the girls home, poured out the schnapps or Wellers or whatever I had. He could read me, O.W., see through the shit.

Maybe we had that in common—seeing though each others' shit.

Trace's wedding reception was at Foxgrave, about close as Mama ever got to her dream wedding, a catered white cake affair after the June ceremony at First Baptist, where those tiny dents up in front of the pulpit marked exactly where Jimmy's casket had sat when I bent over him who linked my heart and blood and love, even, directly to O.W., how he'd bound us together till flying through the windshield at eighty miles an hour on Highway 319 outside Vilonia, the shortcut I'd taught him back from UCA where I'd been the first of us to dare college. And then he was gone and O.W. wept the way he had when his daddy died, and it felt like a heartbreak there is no healing from, one of those moments in life that steals wind from your sails for good and ever. Yes, that was it, Mama's lupus erupting full throttle, and it was only the Clinton Campaign in '92 and the man whose face was so like Jimmy's that stopped her fall, so she'd let her guard down and O.W. had sleuthed it out. Her finalé was set, gone at sixty-one, she drowned of a heart attack he'd said in the midnight call, so we never said goodbye, me and Mama, and for a long time she tried to contact me from the grave until I told her to shut the hell up and die, and she did.

The hot tub leans on its side beside the garage in the back yard, just like I'd dreamed it a half-dozen times. Of all goddamn places, they'd had it installed in Jimmy's bedroom some years after the car wreck, the clothes hanging in the closet just like he'd left them that day before Mother's Day. O.W.'d insisted Trace have it hauled to J'Ville when she uninstalled the monstrosity, and there it sits, the abject tool of my mother's death. Risking all, I pee on it for long as I can, crouched in shadow behind its back, the heat from it enough to melt my hand. Back home, my wife and daughter live their lives, the first of May already, a big ass snowstorm dumping flakes big as hands, a foot of fresh powder gleaming up on Gobbler's Knob.

No such luck here. Arkansas, May, the heat factor brutal already, ninety-five with eighty percent humidity, you forget that in Utah, the heat and the ticks and the fleas. Daddy's air conditioner kicks on, the fan whirring. The pad where he parks his golf cart has oil leaked on it, little circles on top of circles. Odd, in my dream it purrs electric. The back door is unlocked, I walk right on in.

There's a recliner as ever, a brick fireplace and on the mantle the photograph they'd had made without me—the full smug look on his face, *his* family at last, Trace, Mama, O.W. and blue-eyed Jimmy, bad, bad luck if you think about it, letting that picture get taken. And what a twist, here in J'Ville, where Mama'd met my blood father at the Base, his tight-fitting uniform and white teeth—the very town where I'm standing, the family photograph where I'm missing.

Upstairs in his bedroom, the master bath with its scales and poofy toilet cover, Trace's touch, before she moved out with her boy, Dougie, the two of them across town in a trailer park. She'd hit me up over the phone for first and last month's rent. "Mama'd want me to help you," I'd said. "Please don't cry, please."

The way he'd worked it, Daddy, was to mortgage his and Mama's house for all it was worth. It paid off when she died, an add-on they'd signed for when they made the down payment. Then he put the whole load toward 25 Club Road, the property he'd once tried to talk her into buying before she cut him off from the insurance money in her bank account. Our house, Trace signed papers for the full amount, and when she got behind they took it back, she lost the it and had to move in with O.W., just across from Foxgrave, where her now deceased husband and her had cut the wedding cake with a silver knife that shone up front on the cover of her wedding album she's left on the mattress of the bed that must have been hers before he kicked her out, O.W. So the house is gone with Mama's ghost in her dead son's bedroom, a whole lot of skeletons in that closet.

A green chair I recognized sat in the corner of the dark room, an air vent purring in the floor beneath it, the light mute through the draped window—it had hurt her eyes, there at the end, light, Mama. I got down on my knees and crawled behind it, the green chair from home, with nickels and pennies missing from my pockets, Jimmy's under the cushion, bits of food, stray pills. In the house I've never seen but know—what kind of arsonist, me?

Uncle Chester used to call me up drunk and tell me how it happened. I'd be half buzzed myself, so we were on the same channel, me and Chester. I'd take the call in my home office, built on the back of the house's back bedroom, Lara's, and if it was summer, I'd ease open the back door and sit on the steps so the night air would ooze in, listen to him slur how it hadn't been a suicide, it hadn't been like it was for his mother. The most ferocious fight I'd ever witnessed between two men had happened in our driveway when Chester'd called his mother a suicidal bitch. Daddy'd hit him in the face, and then all hell broke loose, both of them heavyweights, over six feet, two forty or so, they beat the living shit out of each other when I was ten or so, and Mama'd had to call the police. She took me inside, but I could hear it through the window, the sound of fist on flesh, I'd never dreamed one man could hit another so hard, both of them bloody-faced, their knuckles dripping. Through the glass, *bap, bap, bap,* that sick sound that stays with you.

He'd helped, Uncle Chester. Taken over O.W.'s rig in Rocky Mount, made the delivery, played his brother to the T. Mama'd never seen it coming, or had she? He'd threatened it plenty.

Trace had found her in the tub a full day later.

Back to his truck, he'd called to say she wasn't answering the phone, that he was worried, how he'd so feared the day she didn't answer his call. I'd been down in Florida that day, June 14, and the call'd come after midnight—Mama'd drowned of a heart attack—how on earth to know that *before* the autopsy? We'd stolen our rental, made the two-day drive to the funeral where he wore the fierce blue suit Mama'd bought him. The grave digger'd called asking where the plot should be dug. *In the goddamn ground,* he'd answered. I'd said that if the gravedigger was a smart man, he wouldn't be a gravedigger, and he'd looked me straight in the face, then turned to Chester. "Dumb truck driver," he'd said, and smiled just a little, which seemed strange to the lost and forsaken soul I was at that moment, me.

"That took a brave man," Chester'd told me the last time we talked. He'd be dead of heart attack himself inside six months, "Standing up there speaking for your mother. I could never do it."

He was sorry about the whole thing, Chester. He wouldn't do it again for anything. Then he died and daddy paid the same funeral home director who'd done Mama to do him. "Oh my," she'd said the moment we met. "You have her skin."

All week in Florida, I'd burned at the beach.

"I've got some cream that will help that."

Hidden behind the green chair from our old living room, the whir of his golf cart, the opening of the back door grounded me in the here and now, cold vent air on the small of my back, dark enough now for the night lights to be on outside. He pissed, long and hard in the first floor toilet. All those years he'd take me in with him to roadside honkytonks, where they'd set me out a Coke in a little icy bottle, a pickled egg or a Slim Jim, and the sawdust from the shuffleboard table shone in the smokey air, everything neon and aglow. Music would be playing, honkytonk blues or swing. I'd follow him to the john that reeked of Pine-Sol and piss, the sugar-sweet aroma of hangover shit. People either loved or feared him. Is there any difference between the two?

Maybe not. I'd always been afraid of him, was only ever comfortable when he was on the road and Mama'd make spaghetti and garlic bread, then he'd walk in and she'd make him a platter and the diesel'd idle all night out on the drive, and nobody'd dare call the cops to complain.

The stairs gave beneath his weight, groaned and creaked. He'd sniff me out. Surely he would. Blood of ancient Cro-Magnon Man in his veins, B-negative, rarest in Arkansas, used in ER transfusions for any type, remnant DNA from the ancient meat-eating hunter. He'd know and he'd stomp my ass, I've come here to die, that's what I thought, and he leaned his head through the doorjamb, sniffed, a little phlegm in his nasal cavities. He could be the stillest man, a snake gazing slit-eyed before the strike. The fear in my throat now, an inch from announcing myself: *I'm here to burn your house down, OW. Go ahead and kill me. Fucker. Do it.*

Then he was gone, and after a while my heart settled some. In my father's house are many reminders of who I am, who I'm not. How I got that way. How much time do I need to consider?

From the door opening into the master bedroom, it's five steps, fifteen feet, to the bed where he lay on his back, face up. Breath rattled some in his chest. Until he got Jesus, he'd been a smoker, Pall Mall, the red package, he'd smoked in bed. Maybe that's how the first house went, him in bed smoking, thick-headed with beer, falling asleep, the butt on the floor, a tissue ignited, then the bed sheets, the whole two-story wood frame gone in an hour, he'd made it out in his underwear, found a hideout key to the Pontiac and driven to

Uncle Earl's down the road. We'd been in California then, and when we got back him and Mama sifted the ashes with a window screen, looking for something or another.

He'd turn eighty on Friday, O.W. His birthday, Mother's Day, and Jimmy's death day all rolled up into one trifecta from hell. Too goddamn much.

In a sweat lodge time and space disappear. Prisoners duck out of jail time when they enter inipi, a portal to the quiet place within. I found out after Mama died when I was sick and lost, and a man I'd only known peripherally had poured a healing lodge for me, channeled Mama's last moments, her voice, even, it came out of his mouth. He'd beat me with eagle's wings, spat in my face, sang the Lakota words to lay the dead to rest, to make them leave you be, a long way, this journey home.

"What did she love?" the medicine man asked.

"Ice water," I said, "Mama loved ice water."

A heavy sleeper, O.W. doesn't budge when I tie his feet to the posts of the very bed where Mama was conceived, that distant time in Danville before the calamities began, not so far from where they'd followed the Trail of Tears down from Henry County, Tennessee, and homesteaded the Solgahatchia bottoms. Where Mama lay now in a field of brown-eyed susan behind the iron gate that squalls when opened.

He does not complain when I tie his hands nor insert the washcloth in his mouth, the silver slice of duct tape across his shaven face, one blue eye opening, and then the other, so he knows, we both know.

There was a time after Jimmy died, when O.W. and I were close—you could say we loved one another—and, like everything else about my people, such manifested itself in ways that bend belief. We were living in Greensboro then. And sometimes O.W.'d roll through in the middle of the night on his way to the drop in Rocky Mount, call us from the truck stop out off the freeway, so we'd drive out to meet him, have a cup of coffee, a piece of coconut cream pie at the Flying J. And this one time, we'd talked about Mama, how hard it had been for her—Jimmy's car wreck and the funeral, the endless string of holidays to remind her of it all over again. Just then, that time daddy rolled in around midnight and rang us on the phone, she was off in Jamaica having the affair that would get her killed, and I believe Daddy'd figured it out, and that he was wondering if I knew, if he could learn anything from me. Hurricane Hugo would plow through that September, barrel right through the truck stop and blow it down. For a while the highway'd close and O.W.'d sleep on our couch and we'd generally get sick of each other for good and ever, but that hadn't happened yet.

We loved each other.

I was his only son.

And of course I had no idea about what was going on with Mama—how could I? And by the time we'd finished with pie he must have been satisfied on that account. He picked up the check, said to follow him to the truck, he wanted to show us something.

Renee had work the next morning—her school, Southeast Guilford had just started and there was a new principal, she had to toe the line.

We were tired. It was past bedtime. We followed him, zigzagging rigs idling in the ten-acre parking lot that was a city unto itself, dealers, prostitutes, a truck for AA meetings and one set up as a prayer chapel. To the idling International, its refrigerated trailer.

He unlocked the padlock, unbarred the doors, climbed up and disappeared into the dim-lit turkey carcasses, the reek of which hit us all at once.

"What's he doing," Renee asked.

I didn't know.

Then he spun on a bootheel, under the garish light of the frozen room, a twenty-five pounder hanging from either hand, that wry smile I'd come to know from the moments when you could tell he was proud of himself.

"Happy Thanksgiving," he said, stepped out and gave each of us a dripping slaughter hen. "Early."

Renee said, "He can't do that."

It was cold to the touch, the bird.

"Oh yes he can."

He nodded—held my eyes with his own. We were on the same page, me and O.W. Those godawful brawls when Uncle Chester called Evelyn *suicidal bitch,* when he'd do all in his power to kill his brother, that was what this was about, standing up for your mother. What was wrong with me? What had taken me so long? Get with it, kiddo. Get her done.

In my rearview, the roof bursts into flame, engulfing the trees and the garage and the goddamned hot tub that leans beside it. The great conflagration roars through the country club and the dipshit driving range, takes aim on the Air Force Base with its endless barrage of cargo planes that rattled our light fixtures during Sunday prayers. Behind me, the whole lot of it goes up, the highest flames to Solgahatchia by now, the sign that says *Welcome to the Authentic Trail of Tears,* a column of smoke and flame you can see from the moon.

They consume the sorry gate's final squall, and it's done.

But, of course, this can't end that way, the movie my mind makes. Hadn't Trace called to say that Daddy'd lost the house, that he was into the final stages of dementia and repeated the same phrase over and over, she didn't know why? It was making her crazy. If I wanted to ever see him alive again, now was the time.

Caught in the fire-eye of my making, I cried out *help me, Jesus, help me,* Renee shaking me to wake, it's okay, everything was okay, wake up now. It's okay.

"What does he say?" I asked her before we hung up that last time, "that makes you crazy?"

"Rock and fire," she said. "I have no clue."

From that place where the paraplegic man lay on his back in deep grass, his teeth shining, recognizing our voices from afar, where were Black Panthers and suicides and *the older you get, the smarter I'll be.* He would have me love him even now?

Rock and fire, O.W.? Rock and fire?

Vows

for Jim Clark

It wasn't the first time we'd stood side by side in front of a priest, me and O.W. I'd been best man in his and Mama's wedding. We'd dressed alike. When he said I do, I said I do. It was a long time ago—a lot of water under the bridge. Now, he'd agreed to return the favor and be first groomsman and best man in our Christmas wedding, the one Renee and I'd planned from scratch after I'd surprised her by handwriting a proposal onto a page of a novel she was reading that fall, which turned out to be the worst luck novel of all time for proposing anything. So we'd planned the ceremony to coincide with a season that had always been a happy time for us—trees and sleigh bells, both our birthdays, wood fires burning into new year's, a clean slate. We'd one day regret the timing, but who knew that in 1987? Eat drink and be merry, and that we by-god did, we went whole hog.

This was the year after Jimmy died. We didn't talk about it at Christmas dinner, after O.W.'d left his semi at the truck stop parking lot and they'd checked into the Battleground Inn up the street, my adoptive father, Mama and my sister, Trace. Jimmy'd been killed on the eve of her Senior Prom. None of us would ever get over it. I was O.W.'s only son now. My heart hurt for him, for all of us.

The two of us wore black tuxedos, maybe the first time he'd ever tried one on. Our boutonnieres matched. His flattop was trimmed high and tight, my hair to my shoulders, I'd always regret it, seeing myself in pictures. To my left, Renee was radiant, the veil powder blue with a hole burned through it from a nervous cigarette. She wouldn't look me in the eye.

We stood there, the three of us, before the Unitarian priest who'd once been the President of NORML, while a saxophone player Renee'd hired played "In a Sentimental Mood," and Mama sobbed from the groom's side first row.

With the last falling notes, the priest lifted his hands for everyone to stand. "Dearly Beloved," he said, so that all hung in the balance that December in the Virginia Dare Room.

Time went holy on me, on us, that's what I thought. Everyone I loved that was alive was there at that moment, on their feet, witness.

Years later I'd learn that she'd decided to say no.

She was scared.

Our road together had wound places she'd not expected, and I was rough around the edges—hell, my edges had edges. I won't go through it all again except to say that exchanging letters with somebody for four years is a lot different than marrying them. You learn a lot about somebody, sure, but not all. And it didn't help for one second that I'd invited the whole rowdy crew from Fayetteville, Arkansas, as if they had something to say about this just for being around on the day we met. Moonshine had mysteriously shown up on our kitchen counter, six half-pint jars, enough to kill a horse, the afternoon the Maid of Honor arrived with her sweet-faced Jewish boyfriend. Ray Ray, two inches shy of being a dwarf, took one look at the woman, said, "Fella, you look thirsty."

"Oh, I am. I'm surely that."

Would he like a sip to take the edge off? Surely it was past happy hour, and they'd been on the road, bad traffic down from DC. Inside of one juice glass, Janowitz was comatose. There'd been hanky panky between Renee's maid of honor and Ray Ray. It got loud in our house. Renee disappeared, and the police showed up shortly thereafter. She spent the night elsewhere, Renee. Years later I'd understand that it had been her that called the police on me and my Arkansas buddies there on Walker Avenue on the eve of our wedding. She'd come an inch from driving away from the whole thing. But her parents were there, they'd paid out their noses already. Dresses had been purchased, and the little blonde flower girl had found one that was an exact match to Renee's antique blue. My people were there, poor Mom Dee in a wheelchair. Not an hour before the ceremony, Renee'd asked Mama if there was anything she should know about me that might keep us from marrying.

"He's just a bewildered boy" Mama'd said.

"Anything else?"

There was champagne in the dressing room, and her mother'd already said that she didn't have to go through with this, she certainly didn't have to. She'd melted a hole in her veil with a Marlboro long.

Beside me, O.W. never said a word. Him and Mama'd married and divorced three times, so it was a mess figuring their anniversary, was it the twentieth? twenty-fifth, the second week of August? First of July? Valentines? But he stood there with me while we waited, solid as a rock. I didn't know what he was thinking, though I have an idea now, how we tend to tally the wrong in our lives at such moments, and hope for the best, that the shadow will pass by and let us live in a good way for another day.

I knew that he was not a bad man to have at my side on such a day, that I'd made a good choice, and, by extension, so had Mama, finally.

It was enough.

I'd never met my blood father, and it turned out that at that very second, about to say vows, the adoption papers from all those years still waited to be certified. I was not who I thought I was, nor the man Renee thought to marry.

We've had time to think about it, to look at it from both ends.

There's a photograph of us leaving the ceremony, guests lining either side of the stairway, pitching fistfuls of rice, though J. Lester, our priest, had warned us that it would swell in the stomachs of pigeons and make them explode. The sun had come out fierce and it's in our eyes, that much is real. We'd spend the night at a downtown mansion, the Blue

Bell Room, which has since, in our tellings, become the Blue Ball Room. Next morning, we ate cold pizza, drove to our home on Walker Avenue where Renee walked into the living room, dragged down our Christmas tree and threw it into the front yard. She told my rowdy Arkies to *get the hell out*, and that's what they did, ducked out the front door into a light rain, and I didn't see any of them again for a long time. Our first day of marriage, we cleaned all day into the night. On my study desk, I found the diploma Mama'd hand delivered, the one that made me the first of my kind to ever graduate. I imagined Mama walking it in through the insult going full throttle, the shine and cigarettes, dope, likely, the hurdy-gurdy of my wedding day. And it never occurred to me for a second that it had been O.W. walked it in, how the rowdies had fallen silent, afraid to blink under his hard gaze.

In time, I'd learn.

Somehow Mama took up with a one-armed man named Lefty, a house painter she'd hired who never got around to painting our house. We'd been married a few years now, me and Renee, and had made the long haul from Greensboro to Lonoke where we'd set a tent in the backyard and sweltered one night, then got up and cooked her breakfast—eggs and sausage from Templeton's IGA down the road, where we hit a deer one far off November night and O.W. got out and finished it with a tire tool, so we took her home and slung it from the little house, and Jimmy and I skinned and gutted before O.W. made chili. She was out of sorts, Mama. O.W., who was just then deadheading home from his Rocky Mount run of slaughter turkeys, had threatened her life, had said he was going to kill her for not the first time. She was afraid, he'd gone cold, O.W.

We were at the table, just inside the bay window where July sunshine was held at bay by heavy drapes, the light hurt her eyes. The house was a mess, really, the bathroom just unbelievable and the bedrooms about as bad.

Beside me, Renee gazed from one of us to the other, that look like when this guy hit a golf ball a few feet from her on the campus course, and she'd slung a nine iron at him: *whacka, whacka, whacka*, the club went.

I said, "Why? Why would daddy want to kill you?"

She wouldn't say, except that he'd met her at the airport when she got back from her Dallas conference, something had made him crazy—who knew with O.W.?

Mama'd end up losing it completely, pulling a ten-inch butcher on him and getting hauled to Charter Vista for a month. I'd talk to her there, how her voice shook— she wanted out. It was a low point, Charter Vista, they stripped her of everything, but, just like her father thirty years earlier, who'd lost a leg in a wood cutting accident and got hooked on morphine, then had to spend a couple months in Boston, getting fitted for a prosthesis and sobriety, she got clean. Mama got right, and she was so proud, getting out, tasting freedom again. What she'd never admit to me in her life was that there'd been an affair with this one-armed man named Lefty, that they'd met in Dallas and O.W. found out. Worse, she'd driven the man to Solgahatchia where, in a field of brown-eyed Susan, Jimmy's State Championship football picture decorated his silver-grey tombstone, overlooking a lightning struck tree and a pond where horses got down on their knees to sip spring water, and blackberry bloomed furiously on every strand of barbed wire. She'd taken this amputee to the place where sons were buried at the feet of their fathers for all the generations since the Stepwells walked down from Henry County, Tennessee. I myself had laid the Stepwell stones around my brother's grave, suffered heat stroke and woke up to the whippoorwills and lightning bugs stinging the air around me, the faint gurgle and splash of bullfrog and smallmouth in the pond, stars whirling above. The horses slurping.

O.W. found it all out.

And after Mama put an end to it, this one-armed Lefty man went back to our family cemetery and desecrated Jimmy's grave. The silver-framed photograph had to be re-epoxied—somebody'd turned it upside down. Would I threaten someone's life for such—someone I loved? Somebody I'd made children with and whose people were now my people? For the desecration of my one blood son's grave, would I threaten the life of one with whom I'd made vows?

Was I my father's son?

I'd discover the photographs the fall after she drowned, neatly arranged for my eyes in the briefcase with its flimsy ass broken lock. I'd thrown them away, a green garbage bag bloated with their smiling faces, but no matter. O.W.'d seen them, and he knew I'd find them when sorting Mama's stuff, that I'd no doubt judge what had happened that hot forsaken summer when I thought I'd die for grief, and it nearly took my family with me, until we made it to Cape Blanco in Oregon, as goddamn far as you can get from the Natural State without jumping in and swimming, and I did that too.

Now, my hotel room faces a fence with concrete stairs leading to a padlocked gate that I climb, hop over to the parking lot that connects to the road up past the coliseum. Left on Chapman to Walker and the home we shared as newlyweds, me and Renee. 9:30 in the morning, it's raining, overcast, but dark enough for glasses. I have two-and-a-half hours until the J. Lester's ceremony, time to make it, I believe. The air is heavy. On either side of the street, closed down businesses, and the ones that aren't closed down sport busted out windows covered with plywood, they've turned into pawnshops with rows of stolen bicycles chained in front glistening with rain. A black man approaches me on the sidewalk. So long in Utah, the sight is strange, and I want to congratulate the man for being here, for walking through my vision.

Far away, the coliseum itself, where I once walked to see the city that followed the Grateful Dead into town, streets with names and residences, people refrying beans and playing banjoes, a woman with yellow hair on a mountain bike, gliding by, saying *ecstasy, ecstasy*, the words lilting from her lips.

Fuck the show, one sign had said, *dose me*.

I cross above Stamey's Barbecue, the all-night pit man walking from the shack where hickory smoke rises from a stack, the sweet beautifully unmistakable aroma of slow-cooked pork rumbling my stomach. The man sees me see him, slaps gloves together, climbs into the truck and lights a cigarette. I'm wet now, soaked through, turning the corner to walk under the wooden railroad trestle, the smell of creosote as a train flies by above, the same whistle exactly I heard thirty years back, down in the place where wind sleeps and somebody's thrown a worn out baby doll with eyes rolled back to the whites, so I speed up a little, come into the light on the other side, awash in a wave of cedar from a plant I've never seen, but know.

A different kind of tree grows here: dogwood, pink bloomed and white, the marks of the savior's wounds hammered into each delicate petal; crepe myrtle with its fuchsia blooms that draw the eye from silky bark to sky, mimosa, which I knew from Arkansas, there'd been one in MaMa Stepwell's front yard, not far from the Chinaberry tree where Mama'd ridden a mini-bike off the ledge and burned skin off her calf on the muffler. Tall trees full of squirrels take the sky so there's a shady greenness, a wet glow, and I'm taking big steps, three feet at a time toward home. Down through the hollow, a front porch bears the photo of an old man. A sign says *In Loving Memory of the Santa of Chapman Street, Daddy, Husband, Brother and Son*, and there's a busted-out manger where baby Jesus used to lay next to a live donkey and Billy goat, a statue of the wise man examining the sky.

The air has a taste to it.

A fine rain mists my face.

I've come to say goodbye, that much I know. To what, I'm not sure. A hundred some of us have flown and drove and hitchhiked here in tribute to the hippy priest who'd married us, a man who'd made a name for himself, who people loved, who'd have moonshine delivered to your wedding party, who knew the ways of barbecue and vinegar sauce. Renee had skipped out—her and Lara in San Francisco right about now, on their way to a Giants game and maybe *dim sum*. *Enjoy the reminiscence*, she'd written in a note folded into my suitcase. *Say hello to the people we knew.*

His daughter, J. Lester's, had been flower girl, and his son was ring bearer—without his family there would have been no wedding. He'd been a friend, the man who wrote our vows, though I never really saw them, scared, hung over beside O.W. I didn't remember a word except there'd been poetry somewhere in those words, and charmed. The priest had called the circle of our space .

Someone found a copy of them cleaning out his office, flew them my way. He'd saved them all these years—thirty—we were lucky for him, our vows had held.

I framed the document, wrapped it for Renee on the day of our anniversary, but she would have none of it, the memory of Arkies still potent, the day simply didn't mean anything she wanted to remember. I can't blame her, I guess, what happened happened.

But Mama and O.W., they'd divorced three times, and some of those times we'd had to run for it, hide out at church people's houses, keep our heads down. Jimmy stuttered, Trace weighed over the top, and me? What did I have to show for all that? There'd been that episode in D.C., the ornament throwing fight one Christmas in Greensboro, that time the police came to our house in Salt Lake.

We'd had a time of it, me and Renee, but isn't that how it is? Love?

It could have gone either way, us. She'd started her own bank account, we'd taken separate vacations. But there was Lara—who loved us equally. We never went through with it. And the thing I never expected in a million years? That it would come to *mean* something to me, really *mean* something. We'd made it, by-god, we had.

Walker Avenue fell away and there it was, the house with the threshold we'd crossed as newlyweds. Both green shutters had been ripped off, so brown rectangles stood oblong beside the picture windows. A building permit was stapled to the front porch, and it hits me that I've dreamed of this place a slew of times and not remembered, of moving back, of running away from Utah and the hinterlands beyond. The front door is cracked. I walk up the five steps, push my front door open.

"Is anyone home," I say.

O.W. broke the cop's nose who delivered papers, hauled off and cold cocked him right in the doorway of the house on Shelley just outside Little Rock. The second time, that was after he burned the house down by accident, nobody knows how all that happened to this day, but it got bad after, living in Uncle's cold-water shack out behind the back pasture. It was the year of the Winter Olympics and Franz Klammer was killing it on the downhill, the giant slalom and slalom. Beneath the bare bulb in our living room, five-year-old Jimmy and I watched the alpine events, and in my dreams it was always snowing, big silver dollar flakes piling house deep, the tin roof our ski jump, I'd let it rip and swear to god I'd go to the mountains when I was old enough to tell them all to go to hell. He disappeared around then, O.W. Mama climbed into bed and didn't get out for two months. I bought groceries with hot checks from the bottom dresser drawer, rode the black mini bike though the woods to the store up on Arch Street Pike. We ate ketchup sandwiches, me and Jimmy. Shit on a shingle. *S—s-s-cinnamon* toast.

The third time had an exclamation point on it, because that's the year we'd all moved to Lonoke, got Jesus, and bought a rent-to-own out in the sticks on this big-ass curve drunks missed so we'd find their cars plastered on the Kentucky wood fence we sometimes burned for cooking. I don't know what happened. He came home crazy one night and threw all her clothes on the back patio, set them afire with gasoline. Mama had me sneak out and start the car. She came running with Jimmy in tow, told me to floor it, which I did. I could hear him behind us on the gravel drive, hollering, he'd have our asses, get back here, I'll kill you. The air was October frosty through the open window. *Son of a bitch, son of a bitch,* I yelled, and it felt good saying that.

There wouldn't be a fourth time. Mama got kind of subdued after Jimmy's car wreck. She needed somebody. Her lupus came on full-throttle, and there were the surgeries. Her death, though sudden, was anticipated.

I gave the elegy at First Baptist, my mouth too close to the microphone so it popped and fizzed through whatever I said. It was just me and O.W. now.

Till death do us part.

The picture windows in the kitchen are busted out and covered, so it's a different kind of light than I remember those mornings when we'd fry country ham and eggs, cut biscuits with a jelly jar, melt butter on the dough. We'd found a puppy down the street, a sweet little black Lab we named Moon—our trial child, so Renee's parents had a bumper sticker that said *Ask Us About Our Grand Dog.*

The bedroom where we took our dinners cross-legged on the floor with the window unit blowing on high cold has some light in it, enough to see inside the ghost closet where hung Renee's prom dress from Southeast, where she chaperoned the dance themed *Stairway to Heaven*, and I was convinced she was having an affair with the baseball coach who recently died, so she pulled his picture up and reminded me of the jealous fit I'd thrown. How I'd waited up and met her in the backyard when she drove up in the Chevy truck with the actual two-by-twelve stairway hulking out of the bed. The stairway to heaven: obscene with glitter glue stars and tapestry clouds, what do you do with such a thing?

The exact spot where we first made love as man and wife, I stand there for a moment and try to recall what it felt like to be young and in love and wild for living. How had we managed? What had held us together these thirty years? There it is, the place where we loved, stripped bare to the floorboards.

I make my way through the dining and living room, out onto the backyard where our garden grew. The crepe myrtle is in bloom, and there's where the ant tunnel went that I'd poured gasoline down into and lit, so little explosions went off all over the yard and we'd laughed ourselves silly for half an hour. A patch of yard near the horseshoe pit grew four-leaf clovers. I'd harvested five years' worth, so a book at home has one dried between every page, hundreds, I'd be giving them as good luck gifts for the rest of my days. A window in the neighboring house is where a woman named Tassie stood naked and smiled at me while I pinched tomato suckers, and once she walked out in a string bikini and joined me between rows, just like she knew my business.

Inside, a four-inch pipe marks the spot where our toilet sat, connected to the sewer pipes of six Walker Avenue bungalows, so that once they all clogged and when the house next door flushed, their shit came bubbling out of our john, and Renee had run out in the yard screaming, "I've had all of your shit I'm going to take."

The raw wood smells of mildew, something else.

It seems unseemly, to be in here, like I've trespassed on some part of myself that is best left alone, some part of us that is over with now, done, complete. They're at the ballpark this second, in San Francisco, Lara's taken her glove for foul balls behind the first base line. She'd never be alone, now, Renee. And we'd forever be connected by blood. We didn't know that about a child then, how instead of *I, I, I, me, me, me*, it becomes about *us*. That's what we'd learn from Lara—what she taught us.

The view from the front porch shines out before me, a little sun coming through the tall trees, roses blooming in the mean lady's yard across the way. I've got the walk back before me, the ceremony at noon where we'll have to look at one another's name tags to know who we are, the year's washing us clean of recognizable traits. How will they know me? I wonder. Renee? Hadn't she come? What would keep her from J. Lester's tribute, the ceremony in the very room where she was married? Hadn't he been our priest? Written the vows with his own hand and heart?

Where was Renee? I'd keep hearing it.

Were we still married?

Damn.

In the space that elapsed before she answered, O.W. and I met eyes. Mama was back there behind us, Mom Dee and Trace, the groomsmen and all of Renee's people. I'd never get a look into his heart, that shadow place where whoever he really was stood revealed. Had Mama ever seen that man. Hidden in my stepfather was the answer to the question Renee'd one day pose: *how on earth can you love such a man?*

We took each other for man and wife, said the vows, and they parted for us to walk through the double doors into the fierce sun. You can't really ever explain this moment to anyone, my own daughter would roll her eyes when I spoke of walking into the derelict house, of standing in the ripped-out bedroom imagining a prom dress and the stairway to heaven. I'd tell her that one day she'd understand what it was like to go back, to feel the fine rain mist your face and breath in the musty breath that held within it the truth of who you'd been, who you were. To take big long steps under the trestle to get there and find the door wide open, a dare or a promise, both.

Maybe that's what I saw in O.W.'s eyes that December afternoon that was my wedding day—go ahead, Joe. Take this walk. I'm with you.

I don't know.

That was thirty years ago. Renee has forgiven that rocky start, if not forgotten. There's a growing up that's happened with time—we're better people, now, I swear. I am. Endings, beginnings, I know.

Hungover and scared—yes, bewildered—I'd never grasped a single word of our vows, not until J. Lester's tribute, when a friend who'd helped clean out his office handed me a photocopy of the original transcript. I remember "Dearly Beloved," but the rest is out of the blue, about Assisi's directive for us to make real the moral dreams that keep us human and whole—

and most of all, we wish for you that at the end of your lives, you will be able to say these two things to each other: Because you have loved me, you have given me faith in myself; and because I have seen the good in you, I have received from you faith in humanity.

The last of it, all of us standing in the charmed circle of our love.

Call Down Fire

A friend of ours got struck by lightning while telling the story of getting struck by lightning. He walked up on our front porch one day carrying a stick. It was a clear day, April, Easter time. He'd been in wilderness therapy, taking rich kids who'd got in trouble out into the wilderness and starving them, making them carve their own spoons. Forsythia blazed all down our street, just like that far off Arkansas springtime when you first knocked on my screen door. Nevada shone out there, the Great Salt Lake. *Do it*, one of us said. He tapped his stick three times to the to the tongue and groove floor, rolled a cigarette, began at the beginning, how they'd been sitting in a circle, just like us now. Five minutes later, bruise-colored cumuli were rolling in from the desert. He lifted his face: *this* light, he said, it's just like *that* light. And whammo, the smell of burned hair, thunder. When he opened his mouth, smoke came out. So I know better. But after thirty years, why not?

I call down fire.

In the afternoon when people quit dying, they let me do features. It was fall, the hillsides all lit up. October nip was in the air. I was twenty-one then, had walked into the *Democrat-Gazette* in Little Rock where I was a minimum wage obituary writer. My desk phone rang that one afternoon and there it was, clean across space and time, your voice. The timbre of your vowels, space between words. Air between the front teeth you knocked out ice skating as a twelve year old, how the hearing loss you inherited from your grandmother would pass to our daughter—you'd grown up hearing songs all wrong, *carry movies home in a jar*, or *look out, Mama, mama there's a white boy comin' up the river*—she'll mix our ashes, cast us to the wind and our dust will mingle forever and ever. I can't tell you how that felt, when I first herd your voice. Like coming home from the road and finding all is well, your mother's Thanksgiving cactus blooming its two colors, wine in the cabinet, light through clean glass and flannel sheets, all is right, no fear, none. We'd fight like dogs, haul off and go at it, say the things that couldn't be unsaid, do the things that couldn't be undone. Who doesn't?

"Hello," you said.

I said, "Hello."

"You're southern."

I said, "I'm in Arkansas."

"I know that," you said.

You were representing the Honorable Beryl Cleopatra, Congressman of Arkansas's Second District. Did I know he'd had two giant watermelons U-Hauled up from Hope, carved them on the steps of the Capitol, passed out t-shirts emblazoned with HOPE MELONS on front?

"Do you know why they call them Hope Melons?"

The phone was blinking, somebody on the other line about to tell me James Daniel Turner died Sunday. He was a Baptist.

"Should I write that? The Hope melons part?"

"Are you a maniac?"

I said, "No. I don't think so."

You said, "Sure."

We exchanged addresses. And those addresses changed about a half-dozen times before we met on an Easter Sunday five years later that coincided with April Fool's Day. When we fell in love and life got crazy.

The last afternoons of our married twenties were spent at a bar down the street where happy hour peanuts were free, and the shells crunched under your shoes on the way to the john. Gib would have been there then, Jim and sometimes Daniele. And you'd come walking in after teaching, your hazel eyes would have that glow, the yellows kindled.

We'd have our red beer and peanuts, talk about what had happened that day and what hadn't, and maybe Jim would tell a joke about how a bird had flown into the local hot sauce factory, and they'd named that batch Carolina Tweet. One time this brain surgeon explained how he'd performed surgery on his grandmother, held her brain in his hands and thought about the memories, her entire accumulated soul there between his palms. The light streamed through the windows and Spring Garden Street was in full bloom. We were still young, and in love, and that mattered. Who knew if we'd make it, misfit loners thrown together by chance. But we'd written five years' worth of letters across space and time—there was *that* foundation. You'd come with me to Greensboro, and said *yes* to my proposal. Your people had driven down for our Christmas wedding in the Virginia Dare Room at UNCG where there was a chandelier and you arranged for the saxophonist—a romantic twist.

We said our vows.

And there we were, arm in arm, stepping out through the double doors where the sun had come out and the glare waylaid us.

Your maid of honor was a general's daughter whose boyfriend drank a cupful of moonshine someone had brought to the house, and he never got out of bed for three days. The general's daughter caroused with one of my groomsmen. My friends had crashed at our house. It happened.

His name was Janowitz, the boy who got sick. They had driven down from Maryland, him and the general's daughter. I'd lent a book to him to read, *The Dixie Association*, and he'd lent it to someone else, and they'd lent it to someone else, and by the time I got it back it was beat to hell.

You threw them all out right after the wedding. The new year was rocky. It was hit and miss. And I hadn't thought of that first pale winter that gushed into spring for a long while, when word came that the priest who'd composed our vows and joined us together, had died. That somehow meant something to our story. We'd been his lucky ones, had weathered the storm called life. And the year was faded to August already, our thirtieth anniversary just down the pike. We'd never had a honeymoon, had we?

The trip was my idea—maybe it would make up for our rough beginning.

Except for Spain, we'd never traveled. So Berlin, and then Prague and Vienna, Paris, finally—that was my idea, you'll give me that. Your grandmother on your father's side, she'd emigrated from Eastern Europe so there was the return to your roots angle, and for that matter I'd arranged to meet with a colleague's friend in Paris. By mid-June we were ready to roll, having put together a list of emergency numbers for Lara who was nineteen then, and had never stayed home alone in her life. We each wrote a will and signed as each others' witness. You left me your flute, and the silver. I left you my deer rifle and boat. If we both died, everything went to Lara.

She drove us to the airport that last morning, hugged us there at the drop off, and drove away, a sweet note tucked into each of our carry-ons. Thirty years married, we flew toward a traveling party of old folks, who were, in fact, only a decade our elders. We flew into night, and then into morning, the windmills gleaming in the English Channel. From my window seat I could see the Eiffel Tower, the shining ribbon of Seine winding toward the sea. Notre Dame, the Arc de Triomphe. You'd raised your brows, said, "What do you see?"

"Paris."

You tried to see around me.

Then the Captain told us to straighten our seatbacks, to prepare for landing. Our shuttle flight to Berlin landed three hours later in a jet-lagged blur. We met our party at a long table in Hackescher Market for wine and meatballs, schnitzel and a first look at our compatriots, dazed and dumbfounded as we were.

To my right, a Jewish cardiologist who played jazz piano on Saturdays in a coffee shop back in Utah. He was old, smiling, seventy-five, maybe. When I asked his name he said, Janowitz, a name I had not heard in thirty years but recognized immediately as the name of the boyfriend who'd passed out on moonshine on the eve of our wedding.

I mentioned his name.

"He's my nephew," Frank Janowitz said. He flashed a picture on his I-Phone. "That's him, right. It's a rare name, Janowitz."

"Renee," I said. "This is Dr. Janowitz. Mark's uncle. From our wedding."

You looked from me to the silver-headed man, tilted your head, so that once again the sun got your eyes. "*No*," you said.

Janowitz leaned forward, held the phone for you to see. And there was Mark, bald now, a shining ghost staring at us from the unimagined past. Or would that be future?

"Yes." he said. "He's my brother's son."

The next day was solstice and the light burst through our window at 4 a.m. Too early for breakfast or wish burning, I walked outside into the quiet city and somehow found the three-hundred-year-old Garrison Cemetery, its wooden gate open. The courtyard was peaceful. Generals lay beside their wives under shade trees, stone crosses bearing their carved names, some of them inlaid with gold, some not. I can't tell you how quiet it was in there. The walls, you could tell they were old, and the light was soft and gold. I was in another country, in a cemetery where men were buried beside women who'd shared their lives, their worst times, their best. I read them one to the next, further and further back to where the sun hadn't shone, these couples bound by life and war and battlements, and now they slept under trees in courtyard shade, high walls to keep out the vandals and dogs. I pictured the windmills turning in the English Channel, you mouthing *what do you see?* and now I was deep into a shady cemetery, to the far wall where the oldest of the generals lay with their long-dead wives, their birthdates intertwined with living lichen and moss, faint to the sight, all in German, foreign, though I had not one bit of trouble understanding the stones, what they said.

Wars I'd never heard of, the shared kiss before battle.

Solstice would come today—three centuries since—and I'd read their names to myself in the new-lit courtyard.

And that exact moment you walked through the Garrison gate, the sun in your hair and your eyes aflame, I'm swearing, that's how you seemed to me then. You'd found your way in, and began to trace my exact path from one stone to the next, and you didn't see me make my way toward you from the shadows the sun hadn't reached. Our first morning in Berlin, a full day in front of us. Solstice—when sun stands still.

I found a wedge of light. And when you saw me you smiled. We sat on a bench in the sunlight until breakfast time.

We'd talked for thirty years. Thirty-five if you count the letters. I don't remember us saying a whole lot that first morning. It was quiet, and the sun felt good.

"What time is it in Salt Lake?"

I didn't know, was it an eight-hour difference? Ten?

"It's not solstice there yet?"

"I don't think so."

"Did you bring wishes?"

Back in Utah, our wills included what should happen to our bodies when we died. We showed each other, and seeing it in words made it real. We'd signed the printed pages in blue ink because that's the color they'd made us sign for our house so that seemed right, sealed them in envelopes and left them in the top drawer of Lara's desk, with the emergency numbers and bank books. We scribbled wishes on notebook paper for her to burn along with her own. Burning wishes on Solstice, good mojo. Across the ocean where she slept.

How'd you sleep?" You'd showered already, dressed for the day.

I said, "Good."

We walked out the gate together, found the revolving hotel door and coffee and breakfast, eggs three ways and five kinds of ham, apples and strudel. Our travel mates arrived in pairs, grey hair combed and shining.

From the top of the Reichstag, one has a 360-degree panorama of Berlin, the wide swath of green that marks park and river, to the concrete block memorial for the murdered Jews, the grey slabs bleeding one into another from the distance. There was the Brandenburg Gate separating East Germany from West, and a little further into the shade a memorial to the Gypsies who Hitler'd wiped off the map, coins in the little reflecting pool glaring and dressed up kids conning tourists out of email addresses and names, birthdates.

Back on the ground, you'd found ice water. Cool and sweet, you poured some down my back, yours.

"Most tourists," the guide said, "Think this is only a place to park bikes."

He rested his hands on one of the ninety-six metal plates, cut and welded together with little slots just right for bike tires, a whole slew of them, they were rusted in places, worn slick in others.

"Look," he said, pointing.

Writing shone on top of each, dates, places of birth and death, concentration camps, Auschwitz, others. He told us how in 1930, Adolph Hitler won plurality without a majority with the Socialist Workers Party—the Nazis. He wasn't popular. When the president died, he had himself made president. He consolidated power. The politicians thought they could use him, that they might cling to power through him. They were wrong. He passed the Enabling Act which made him immune to all laws. He had all Jewish lawyers disbarred. He murdered 96 members of Parliament who opposed him. Here were their names, where and when they died. "By ninth grade, we all have to learn this. Maybe you learn too," he said.

Sure enough, warm to the touch, ninety-six metal plates. It was the year Trump had won the election back home. He wasn't popular. He made himself immune to laws, to impeachment, even. He consolidated power. The Republicans thought they might keep power through him. The shit had hit the fan—who knew what was coming? We stood there for a minute, sipping ice water. All those names. It was hot, not a cloud in the sky. Over there was Check Point Charley, a display called the Topography of Terror. The guide took off walking, we followed.

I entered the Jewish Memorial on my own, this whole city block with slabs stood upright as pillars, block upon block upon block of grey concrete, the sun glittering on one side, shadow on the other, a maze where you'd run into people all of a sudden and get disoriented and not know the way out because everything looked the same, which was I guess the point. I made it out, somehow I did, crossed a street to what I'd learn was the unmarked site of the fuhrerbunker, where I sat in the shade of a closed Italian restaurant, smoked, and watched our party emerge from the jumble in ones, and twos, some swiping at their faces. And I thought of Lara at home alone, feeding the chickens, walking the dog, the sound our refrigerator made when the ice maker dropped cubes in the middle of the night. Maybe I said a prayer for her then, dwarfed by the concrete city block, where everything ran into one thing, and you walked out then.

I was glad—that you'd made it out.

You didn't see me. And I hadn't yet thought that all those blocks, they stood for people who had families, wives and husbands and daughters, sons. I watched you from the wedge of shade under the canopy of the shut-down Italian restaurant not a rock's throw from where Hitler married his mistress Eva on their last morning, where they said vows, kissed before putting bullets in their heads.

Under the brilliant hot sun, you opened your mouth and spoke, as did each member of our group—what had it been like in there? How did it feel to you, wandering in the memorial to six million slaughtered?

The swords of executioners have no points.

I learned it at the Museum of German History, where, out of the blue, Henry Kissinger spoke from a podium on the 70th Anniversary of the Marshall Act. We wandered in and separated, you to the paintings of pot-bellied monarchs with their ridiculous moustaches, me to the swords, implements of battle, the changing maps of Germania, crucified Christs with blood running from the seven wounds, everywhere a Madonna with child. Santiago posed with his scallop shell and staff, about to walk across Spain.

I found you sitting on a bench in the Portrait Gallery not far from Louis the XV, Sun King. Our feet were killing us. We retraced our way to the TV tower that marked the hotel next to the military garrison where the wives and husbands slept root entwined under trees behind the courtyard gates. We closed the curtains to our room and threw ourselves into bed, slept afternoon till night in the cool, sweet dark. Then we rose together, slipped on something and walked outside into the night, turned a corner to a Korean place with tables outside. We ordered, took a table apart, the lights of Berlin and a lone candle flickering, held hands for a moment. No, really. Our food came and it was the first time we'd eaten that way together in a long time—young almost, in love. We toasted, dined on marvelously fried chicken and spring rolls, sweet summer wine. We each burned a single wish. The moon was out.

Wasn't it nearly full?

One whole summer I hauled hay in Lonoke County. We lived in a house trailer on the skirts of our landlord's pastures cut by four-mile creek where I'd trapped rabbits winter until spring, cut one open and these pink hairless babies fell out. Way out in the country near Mountain Springs where Cherokee lived on the remnants of the Trail of Tears. Mr. Guess, the landlord, had a son who lived in a trailer next door to him—he had the palsy or something and couldn't talk, really, or walk, like he'd locked up from the inside out. His name was Paul, and he'd married a woman, from his school, I guess, that suffered the same affliction, so she'd be beside him, holding one of his hands, her mouth locked in answer to his own.

That was 1975, so I was fourteen, had just won the track medal for junior high, in a race off with a Cherokee boy named Mayfield, who I'd eventually live with for a while when mama went to the facility and O.W. was off in Florida getting sober.

Mr. Guess cut hay twice that summer. Paul and his wife would slow drive a pickup in this huge square where the bailer had spit out bails, and I'd pick them up by the hay rope, throw them up to Kenny Skinny, Old Man Guess's other hay recruit, and he'd cross stack them on the trailer, which was tricky because of the two tires, one on either side, so you didn't want to lean in front of one when hoisting up a bail. Which is exactly what I did on an afternoon after lunch and Ms. Guess's Iced tea, leaned in front of the right front tire and got sucked under and run over in the pasture that skirted four-mile creek where an Indian boy'd taught me to trap the rabbits we lived on until mama was taken away.

Kenny Skinny screamed at Paul to stop, and Mr. Guess's son came hopping and scrunching up to where I lay. His wife was behind him, crying. Are you okay? Are you okay? he tried to say.

For the rest of my life, the smell of mown hay takes me to that moment, when I lay runover in the hayfield under a blue sky, my brother and sisters up in the house trailer where mama was in bed moaning, I never knew why.

Are you hurt? Paul Guess's wife tried to say, and I felt her hand on one shoulder, her tremor run through me.

From where the trailer had sucked me under, run me up the middle, I saw shining bales spit out in haphazard rows, the nearest one with a sliced-in-half king snake gleaming from the upside, and further off a truck *thunka thunked* across the creek bridge heading our way. I'd later learn that it was daddy come back from Florida, thin and sober, ready to have another go. We'd move into Lonoke City in two weeks, Mountain Springs would be history.

A third time Guess asked me. Hot August, the heat shimmied like gasoline rainbows from there to Dead Man's Curve. Witch doctors flew by in twos, their hooked tails fierce green. The praying mantis lifted off its eggs, a tornado forming near Fordyce that would suck our post office into the sky, send our mail off in the jet stream to Canada, the arctic, the moon. This beautiful hard country I'd grown up in, thirsty, allergic to hay, and the silver band of creek winding north toward Conway and R-Ville and Mt. Nebo, the highest point in Arkansas.

I said, "Can I drive the truck. If I'm okay, can I?"

Paul shook his head about fifty times and his wife's mouth locked into a bright smile. They got me up. He showed me how to work the column gear shifter, and for the rest of the afternoon I drove squares into the land while Paul and his wife worked either side of the Chevy, lifting hay bales up to Kenny Skinny who cross-stacked them until they were over his head and the day was done.

"Look," you said, the road rising into sloping hells between Dresden and the Czech Republic. "They're making hay."

You had your own row of seats behind me. The rest of our bus dozed, poking their phones with ear buds in and blinds pulled.

Huge bales were being lifted by a tractor with a front-end loader. I cracked the window so the smell came in, and there I was back home, only you were with me now. And I knew somehow from both places that everything'd be okay, that I'd make it out alive, and that my life would be alright. I'd find love, be blessed with a daughter. Mama and the rest, I couldn't save them, but I'd get out free.

You smiled, sipped from your water bottle.

"Almost there," you said.

The Hapsburg emperor built Terezin as a fortification against invasion, and named it after his mother, Teresa, who he loved. Our leader arranged this visit to the concentration camp just over the border of the Czech border sight unseen. He'd never been there, though I guess he'd heard the stories, maybe even seen the movie clips of the city Hitler supposedly prepared and gave to the Jews. About the misshapen *B*, the monthly trains to Auschwitz. I know he hadn't heard about the trove of children's drawings, nor the art museum of forced art, the crematorium nor cemetery. Neither of us had done our homework either. We'd stumbled off behind our guide—*Vida*, *life* in Spanish—like sheep to the slaughter.

Here's how I see it: the compound is walled, way the hell out in the country with no stores, hardly, gas stations, and it's a sunny day, bright and shining, and you're sitting behind me in the deluxe bus with its crushed velvet seats and unused toilet and self-directed air and seat temperatures, and our driver cruises us through this gate with *ARBIET MACHT FREI* printed in big red letters around the curve of the arch, only the B's misshapen, the upper lobe swollen, not much, just off-kilter enough to see that the hands that forced the letters knew the lie.

We parked at what looked like a soccer field, it was just the right size, and the grass was so green. All the buildings looked the same, brown brick, wood frame windows, glass panes shining in this way that turned me around.

"Let's do this together," you said, or I imagine you saying, and for the rest of our time at Terezin Ghetto, we stayed together, if not holding hands, almost.

It was chilly, and you'd put on the white sweater I'd never seen before. Your hair shone against it, your eyes. Vida led us into a building with a theater which had been the school for imprisoned children. And since this was to be Hitler's showcase lie, a manifestation of his feigned good will toward the German and Czech Jews, here were imprisoned the artists and musicians and famous writers, the philosophers and actors and poets, the very finest painters and architects and doctors and lawyers, people who had been somebody, who'd possessed wealth and prestige and dignity and, yes, for many, family—sons and daughters and mothers and fathers and wives and husbands, partners and significant others, and the whole bloody lot of them were on their way to the special stop at the far gate that led to Auschwitz-Birkenau or Treblinka or, if the disease and starvation got them here, the ovens, as we would see.

We waited in a room hung with old movie posters, an exact replica of Terezin with little lights that lit up when you pushed buttons that said Men, or Women, or Children or School, hidden synagogue or hospital, fake soccer field, mass grave.

Then a door opened and Vida ushered us into an empty theater that was dark and chill and we took a seat up front, just to the left 10:30 in the morning, maybe, and I could smell your hair, the shampoo you'd used that morning back in Dresden, where it had rained big beautiful rain and the world felt new.

I forget the name of the film, but not the details. Terezin bloomed in springtime, so many flowers gushing, and the pictures from the bakery of fresh baked bread and the camera panned to healthy jews working in tomato gardens, the exquisite lettuce and cabbage, cut to the symphony, Chopin so sharp it carved the brain with the lilts and turns—all of the beautiful people in their fine suits of clothes, dancing, their mouths smiling. The children acted in their holiday pageant, bowed to thunderous applause and more mouths made into smiles.

Hitler, the world was to be told, had built a city for the Jews, to protect them from the vagaries and stresses of the war. Two hundred thousand men, women and children passed through the gate with its misshapen B as a waystation to the East and death. The film showed the mythic city where came the doomed from nine nations. There was a voice. It was English. There were candy shops. Bon bons and Viennese chocolate.

The Red Cross had been invited. There were famous composers, a children's operetta. And finally, there was a soccer game.

The men were beautiful, uniforms crisp, their cleats throwing turf when the ball crossed one to the other, worked in the triangles I'd learned from coaching Lara and the girls on fall afternoons when the light shone on the Wasatch and the leaves were going orange and yellow. The light was on your face—it flickered.

Wild applause from the crowd at the home team's goal—who were the opponents exactly of these broad-shouldered men, the lithe half back and dark-headed middle defenseman? Glorious winners in the end, emblazoned, the crowd on its feet, one of the Home Team heroes lifted onto shoulders, the Nazi guardsmen with their Gestapo-issued 45s and cattle prods nowhere to be seen, every prop's arrival and departure perfectly transparent.

The Red Cross had reported that life at Terezin was acceptable, that Hitler was doing his best. "This is making me sick," you said.

Outside the theater were paintings of the real place, and we had not prepared to be so brutally undone. The children's drawings, a sled flying away on snow. Finally, on the walk to the crematorium, site of the mass burnings, we bailed, walked to the bus and drank beer.

The doomed inmates had painted the lopsided B—work did not set them free, and the grain of truth in the lie was enough to kill you.

Later, Prague was castle and river and courtyards where ten-thousand tourists reveled all night long, the footbridge over the wide gleaming water crossed and recrossed till sunrise, when the painters came to capture the light. Gathered at the bar across our street, the all-night revelers huddle, smoke. One of them laughs. Today is Saturday. I wonder for Lara, how is it for her an ocean apart. The hotel was very old, had been a brewery since 1466. The ceilings were high, ten, eleven feet, maybe, and the light was good through the open windows, a chill in the air, and they were singing across the street, the twenty-somethings, passing lit cigarettes, running hands through tangles, and I watched you sleep, the light just touching your face, and again I felt what it means to love deeply, to make a child together, a life, how it must have been for those families, not at all unlike us to walk through the arched gate with its misshapen B, to be separated, women *there*, children *there*, men *there*, forbidden to see or touch each other, to hear one another's voices. Imagining the holiday pageant, distinct voices ringing from the false operetta, the drawing of a sled ridden breakneck away drawn by a child who walked into a gas chamber holding his mother's hand, a thin bar of white soap in the other because it was a shower they were taking, only a shower before bedtime. And these sentient beings—what had they thought at the moment of truth? When they breathed gas. When they dropped the soap. Had they met eyes? Said I love you.

Last thought in life, first thought in death.

In the courtyard under the open sky, we ate crepes. Our leader stuck his head out a window and laughed. We'd changed all our money to crowns, which you called cronins, for some reason. The 6'1" guide with a pixie haircut and purple umbrella, Linka, led us though the Castle of Wenceslas, and we stood together in the Great Hall which was eighty meters long with intricately laced ceiling joists above a parquet floor. Light poured through the windows, splashed on the hard wood. They held jousts in here, of all things. A two-foot ledge ran around the entirety of the space, for knights to step onto so as to mount horses. I pictured them running under such a roof, the amazing clatter, colors, unseatings, blood.

We found Kafka's house.

The door was small. Number twenty-two, painted blue. I bought two postcards for Lara, which the sweet woman at the front desk of the hotel would mail, though I didn't see the stamp until two days after we returned, when the card arrived and Lara walked it out to me, weeding in the garden, a hundred and three degrees, maybe: a beautiful woman with a flower garland around flowing red hair, a necklace of silver crystals, framed in a rose window, Ceska Republika.

But finally the day came down to doing laundry, just like thirty years ago, when we'd drag our bags into Suds & Duds, separate whites from darks and make change at the bar, order sudsy beer from the tap, and wash our clothes on Sunday afternoon with football on strung up TVs, and the light from outside really did have the heft of cathedral tunes.

No Suds & Duds, we walked huge squares into neighborhoods where the front desk clerk who drew two mugs of keg beer from behind the front desk had told us a laundry existed. We walked and walked and walked, and yes, we argued. Our backpacks were heavy on us—two weeks of dirty underwear.

Finally, you turned a corner and there it was, beside a bar, the change machine broken, a troupe of hostel boys stuffing sleeping bags into all the dryers. No one would make change, not in the bar, nor the market next door. Making the soap machine work was beyond us.

That night we lay in bed and watched soccer. Maybe it rained, the cool chill and the sound of it falling on the window sash. Had we made love, the downpour emptying the streets of revelers? Had we held each other and listened to rain and the sounds of chefs cursing and laughing in the restaurant below, the seasonings reaching us in the night?

If not, I wish it so.

After a night in Ceske Krumlov, a mountain town with a shining river where kayaks were rented without life jackets, where we ate fresh trout riverside and walked the steep path to the castle so real it seemed fake with its overlook of town and river at sunset, a night when bright Saturn shone straight above the castle spire, and the air through our open windows was brisk and filled with bells at sunrise, when we sipped beer with the locals at the brewery—one with palsy, another cross-eyed, and the third drunk and mumbling. Vienna was a dream, its pancake houses and Albertina, the Treasury, a giant carved emerald formed into a host for communion wine, a unicorn horn cut from a Narwhale, the crown once worn by Charlemagne, the finest on earth with pearls and rubies, gold and silver and diamond—I looked at it close up, behind the glass, the light crazy on it. We met eyes, you leaned over the crib made for the child of Napoleon and Josephine, and in the next room shirts of the Order of the Ram, clothes so fine, it was claimed, that the makers went blind in the making.

Our last meal in Austria was Schnitzel, carafes of wine, and for the first time, we dressed for dinner. Our company sat at a long table, and the woman at my side was drunk, had forgotten half the trip. After, we walked past the Opera House, the Austrian flag flapping on a pole, one high note lost in vibrato.

The stars were the same—Vega high up, pale Lyra, the summer triangle.

June was over, the season fading.

The flight to Paris was insufferable. The seats were crammed together, and there had been turbulence. Someone had screamed. *Goddamnit*, I remember them saying, the stewardesses canceling beverage service, lashing themselves into seats front and back. We sat close to each other. It was light outside, some clouds, and the airplane bucked, felt for the world like it was falling from the sky. You sobbed, started deep-breathing like the nuns taught you when we practiced for Lara's birth, when we were the best breathers in the C-wing. We held hands then, breathing. One breath, another. People could think what they might. Comfort in this world, when we're scared or hurt or dying of grief or affliction—is that what love was, finally, to need and give comfort?

The hotel you'd chosen was a good one. A veranda overlooking a busy square not far from the Louvre, these restaurant bars packed with young people who smoked and drank beer, hit on each other, and did not know what the future held for them any more than we had.

That first night in Paris we walked for dinner, ate outside where a candle burned and a couple danced in the street. *Une petit opportune*, the name of the restaurant. Lights shone from heavily draped windows, and we got lost finding the way back. We slept the sleep of the dead, rose up to descend the spiral stair to a basement with brick arches and a machine that squeezed fresh oranges, awful eggs and uncooked bacon. The finest buttered croissant I've ever put into my mouth.

In the Louvre were fifty-yard-long scrolls of papyrus covered with magic writing to protect the dead on their journey, these unbelievable paintings of serpents and dogs and birds to guide them through. The sarcophagi were painted with novels of narrative on each surface, the wooden ones and the stone, carved with every imaginable ceremonial thought. The body lay on impeccably glyphed angels and serpents, birds of prey, and we turned a corner where the light ceased abruptly, focused intensely on a corpse posed so elaborately as to defy words. The stillness of the thing, the human shape beneath shield and wrap forever and ever. We stood before it, thirty years married, human.

Out under the blue sky, we drank the air and light, found the veranda and devoured our wine and ham and salmon and cheese, a fresh baguette. We drank and smoked while it got dark in Paris, walked to the river and found a spot for cognac before bed on our fourteenth night out. We called Lara. Before you asked me to turn the light out on the day, we called, heard her voice, that she missed us.

She said *I love you.*

A cold rain fell on our last day, a Sunday, the sky hard like wind on water. Folk walked by in parkas, scarves whipping. We walked to Notre Dame, waited in this long curving line, and it wasn't until we were inside that I realized Sunday Mass was going on, a priest leading the ceremony, light streaming in through thousand-year-old stained glass, the singing, an altar boy swinging the silver bowl with smudge smoking out in clouds. We breathed it in, paid our two dollars, and lit the candle near the tomb of a saint, prayed for safe passage, gave thanks, breathed our daughter's name and left it burning. A thousand years—*Our Mother.*

Breath steaming before our faces, we walked the bricks under the Arch de Triumph, smelled the flowers that lay at the foot of the unknown soldier, found the Seine, wind whipping our hair, sun low and golden, now.

As if summoned from dream this glass boat sailed upriver, its platform filled with a wedding party in full dress. There was a jazz band, and the music washed over us, the horns, drumbeat, the tremolo. On the bow, in brilliant white, the bride and groom stood arm in arm on a platform, the gauzy dress fluttering in the wind, her hair a sheet of light, cameras flashing. The party cheered them. They leapt, the two of them, their hands linked above as if in victory, light splashed across their faces as they fell.

In the photograph of us in Paris, the Seine behind our backs, the glass boat shimmying down river, our hair is crazy with the wind. We look into the camera together, as if to say we've made it. After a lifetime messy with living, the exhilarate heights and bleak separations, here we are, in Paris, very much in love, see, that's what our faces say. *See?* The Eiffel Tower's back there, Notre Dame, the bride and groom embraced midair, their leap never fully over. See our faces. The *good* in our faces. There on the river, the water ever flowing behind us, never the same way twice. I love you. I always have.

We stumbled back into a Hari Krishna gathering in a square with a fountain where they fed us heaping bowls of rice and potato, spice and cilantro, very good, and on stage a troop of them were singing, a girl dancing before them—her hands, eyes, feet, smile, little sister beside her, my heart, soul touched by them again, the Haris, like that first month in DC when they fed us at the Capital, 4th of July, thirty years ago now. What were they thinking? Feeding us for nothing.

And that little girl, her smile, the way she looked at us when the music stopped, the way she held her hands out. See? *See?* We flew back over the Atlantic to a layover in Chicago, delay after delay after delay, until the touch down in Salt Lake after midnight. Our Lara was there to meet us with a handwritten sign, salted caramel, she drove us into the cool mountain night where stars I could not name burned overhead and went on burning. Home, something had melted in the dishwasher, the smell of it touching a thought I'd long since driven away.

Sebastian Rising

The elderly were doing it. *Live while you're alive*, the island folk were saying, going nude in the surf. Mid-eighties, Renee's father had wed the township's Aussie hairdresser on Valentine's Day at low tide under a flower-laced arbor, then poured out twenty-six cases of Tott's champagne for the beachside hootenanny that followed. *Florida Today* ran a story that pinned the funny business on the cult of St. Sebastian, whose historical representations had inspired carnal thoughts in men *and* women, and for whom the island's Episcopal Church—and a dozen other landmarks—was for some reason named. There was historical precedent, the story went. Now, the old man was fading. The last time we'd traveled to Florida, Renee and her father'd wept bitterly in parting, sure they'd never see each other again in this lifetime. Like me, she'd missed the chance with her mother—they'd never said goodbye.

The tang of ocean hit us over Eau Gallie causeway, where white buoys marked crab pots wired with yesterday's fish heads. Last fall's hurricane had taken the concrete dragon, but the point remained, a trio of pelicans riding out the breeze. Indialantic, the boardwalk, we powered the rental's windows full down, breathed it in. Red-eye from Salt Lake to Orlando, one day had bled into another. The three of us. South at the light, blue surf flashed between tall hotels and condos with their water-stained drives and swaying palms, lawns one good storm away from the seagrape and bayonet that threatened from the bush. Indian River on one side, Atlantic on the other. Turtle tracks shone against the dunes. The sun rose up out of the ocean, full and clean.

We'd been abroad that summer, Renee and me, and there was still that off-kilter feel of using strange toilets at 3 a.m., the sliver of hall light under doorways where halls wound to elevators and rubbish shafts, emergency exits. Renee'd found a false eyelash in a Vienna sink.

Best not fuck around on Oak Street. Thirty miles an hour, and the man means it. Find yourself shoveling shit at Sheriff's Farm like Rocky did, Renee's younger brother, married for a second time down on Sixth Ave.

Cap's martini flag was flying. The grass was fresh-mown and the trash barrels had been pulled in. I hauled our suitcases out of the trunk and the three of us made a line to the front door, like the time Cap'd had a heart attack and then a stroke, and we'd flown down for Easter with six-month old Lara. Like the summer when I'd flown in with four surf rods and Cap had run over them with his truck and pretended it hadn't happened.

Like when Renee had met him at the door after Meg died. Like when he'd flown us in on Christmas Eve for the Feast of Seven Fishes and gone down on one knee to propose to Rose, a widower, a diamond ring bright in his good hand. Now, they'd all got frisky—*Live While You're Alive*, the *Florida Today* headline had read.

Cap was feeding the cat in his skivvies. The TV was on. It was Monday morning, a clean slate. We walked right in, pulling our bags behind us. Outside the sliding glass, the pool was the same as ever, the boat shed and banana trees, the stretch of curved sidewalk I'd poured one godawful hot July. The cat was huge and fat. Back when Meg was alive, it was a neighborhood stray, munching palmetto bugs and drinking pool water. Rose had let it in when they were newlyweds. Now the son of a bitch meowed like he owned the place.

There was a moment of confusion when he looked up and saw us, like he was surprised we'd come. Then they hugged, father and daughter. "How was the flight?" he asked, pouring cat food from a bag into a shiny bowl.

"Fine," Renee said. "Is that Mom's silver?"

"Look at you," he said to Lara who was nearly big as him now. They'd planned a tag-on trip at the end of ours, taking the car up on the Auto Train to D.C. and seeing the sights, driving one last time over to New Jersey to tell the farmhouse where he'd grown up goodbye.

Just then walked in Rose, her hair done and shining. "I want to show you my bathroom," she said. "You're not going to believe the bathroom."

Renee and Lara followed her into the master bedroom. Meg's piano was gone. The new TV was on *Treasure Coast News*.

"Any trouble?"

We started to shake, then hugged. A Navy captain, he'd lost weight, but he was still there, eighty-five now, not yet frail.   "We couldn't figure out how to start the car."

He smiled. "That happened to us. In Delaware."

Rose led Renee and Lara in raving about the remodel, how they'd tripled the size of the shower so they could both go at once. She smiled. "You have to use it, Joey. The pressure's great. Have you had coffee?"

We sat at the island, retraced the contours of what we knew to talk about: Rocky, his new wife, the kids, Rose's son who was always on the cusp of marrying, but never did. His dog. Our lives in Utah. Lara's first year of school. How the new president was crazier than a shit-house mouse. Dinner. The guest room paintings were all different. Where an oversized picture of Rocky had been was an Aborigine piece of interlaced fingerprints. The bookshelf was gone, all the family photographs. They'd installed a window unit—the cold knocked us sideways. Then we went to bed and slept till three, Lara conked out on the makeshift bed Rose had set up for her in the Florida room.

My dream was a jumble, a snippet of the airplane movie, Mama dressed as a flapper. St. Sebastian shot full of arrows, that look on his face. In Berlin, then Prague, and then Vienna, we'd walked museum floors on swollen feet and viewed the paintings, different renditions city to city, but Sebastian was always among them. I hadn't bothered to learn his story, not until we got back and I heard the news from Florida. How he'd been a Roman soldier who was found out as a Christian, and his commander had him tied to a stake. They used him for target practice, the bows singing. The Old Masters painted golden light pouring down on his anguish, his last breath. Only, when this maid came to wash his body for burial, he lived. The arrow riddled man breathed though he'd *surely* been dead—water in his blood. So this maid, whose name was Irene, a widower, she took Sebastian home and nursed him to health. By the 1600's he'd been elevated to sainthood, and his story became a favorite, the promise of life for those who are honorable in death.

It was a good story, Sebastian rising.

"Any longer you'll miss goddamn happy hour," Cap said through the door, the sound of ice tinkling.

Our second full day on the island dawned clear, a little breeze early from the river side, the cold, clear sea water a delight to the flesh and blood. I'd waded out fifty, seventy-five yards in a falling tide, a pod of dolphin zinging the baitfish and a white sail lofted out on the blue curve of ocean. Treading water, there was Sand on the Beach Lounge, and the rich people's condos up the curve toward Satellite and Cocoa, and finally Canaveral, where humankind blasted off to take the moon. It was the best time, really, sunrise at the beach, no one around save the walkers who bent now and again for a shell, a feather, sea birds charging and retreating from the surf. A lone blue heron stood on one leg staring into waves with stone eyes. 6:30, not 7 yet, I'd ridden one of the bikes that had air in its tires up the street to 3rd Ave access, where you could view the panorama, see how the day was panning out. If it had been high tide, the surf fishers would be there, going to town on whiting, pompano if they were lucky, but the tide was low. I'd slipped off the pair of Chaco sandals I'd worn across Europe, and before that while rowing the Grand Canyon, left them on a wooden step, walked to the water, stripped and waded into the heavenly chill. They'd moved here in '93, Meg and Cap, the year we'd moved to Utah. A long time, a lot of water under the bridge, and then Meg had died, and we'd come for the funeral, and after walked the ocean to a place where it stayed dark all night long, so the sea turtles swam in to lay eggs in the lightless stretch of dune. Renee had taken it as a sign, the mother turtles swimming in, their last words, her and Meg.

Rose had come out of thin air. Who could predict such?

And she'd been the island's hairdresser, had done Meg's hair for God's sake, and knew the dirt on everybody and anybody in the small township of tanned Floridians, moneyed folk who knew how to live, who valued the good things in life. She'd sold her house, moved in with Cap, and stayed after him to remodel up one side and down the other. Stucco over the wood rot, recarpet, let the good times roll.

Renee's brother, he'd finally managed a divorce from his fire-breathing dragon of a wife, and the adopted kids had grown into handsome young beach rats with Smart Phones and thousand-dollar surfboards. He'd remarried a woman ten years younger but you really couldn't tell, Rock was in good shape for mid-fifties. He had a new boat, a twenty-six-foot Boston Whaler, and we'd arrived on the eve of lobster season. There was talk of a surf and turf, the whole family together again before the sojourn north to DC and the final farewell to Cummings Road.

Sometimes Renee'd appear at the top of the stairs—the moment I thought of her, there she'd be. Only today, it's this guy on a Stingray bike. Even from a hundred yards I can tell he's homeless, one of the vagrants who hang behind the drug store and live by stealing whatever they could finagle from the beach crowd who show up day in day out with leather wallets full of cash, coolers of iced Coronas and salami, good cheese, stuff. He saw me see him, raised one hand above his eyes, saluted me I'm swearing to God, reached down and slipped a finger through each of my Chacos, and rode away. He'd never even gotten off the Stingray.

By the time I got out, he was long gone. A cop at the overlook said he hadn't seen anyone on a bike but me, looked at me sideways.

I pedaled up to Cap's house, washed my feet in the pool and walked inside. Lara was still zonked out, only she'd moved from the Florida room to the couch in the living room. Renee'd made coffee. She said, "Your cup's over there."

I said, "A guy stole my Chacos."

"Do what?"

"My sandals," I said, and Rose walked in, dressed for work. "This guy took my shoes at the access."

"Your shoes?" Rose said.

"Hundred-dollar Chacos."

It was Tuesday. For tomorrow we'd planned to drive over to Tampa for a Ray's game, our first time at the Majors. What in hell do you do in Florida without sandals?

"You should've kept 'em with you. You know better than that," Renee said. "Will you have mango?"

Lara got up from the couch, raised her brows, gave me the look.

I said, "It's nothing. Just my shoes."

The cat arched its back and hissed. Outside, a squirrel gnawed a shell under the statue of St. Francis of Assisi. The day was just starting. It was going to be a hot one. A scorcher. I'd rowed Lava Falls in those shoes. Fastest navigable white water in the Western Hemisphere.

"They crawled on me." Lara whispered it. "On my face. Those bugs."

Cap had bought tickets to the Rays game in Tampa, probably to get us out of his and Rose's hair. They had business. We cramped their style. "There's four here," Renee said. "You want to come?"

"Have fun," the old man had said. "It's our night out."

We raided the pantry and drove away, air on high, Tom Petty belting "American Girl" with bass overtones. A bevy of bikini clad ladies were crossing Main Street behind canes and walkers, followed by an old man in a Santa hat and Speedo, surfboard tucked under his wrinkled arm.

"Cool," Lara said. "Do you think you'll be like that?"

Renee said, "No."

A green-eyed mannequin was bent over a bench at the Burrito Bar—her blonde wig glowing in the morning sun with the far-off blue exaggerating those eyes. A guy who'd once been a fashion model ran the place, and the mannequin was always there, bent in some new position.

I said, "Maybe."

Lara said, "Live while you're alive."

The Rays had a catcher named The Buffalo, and everywhere flapping around Tropicana Field were these signs that said *Trust the Buffalo*, with a picture of this bull-chested man giving you his *I'll cut your nuts off* look. Inside was this huge glass aquarium filled with silver stingrays, their skinny tails flicking inside a wall where a whole section of seats was guaranteed free pizza and beer if a home run dropped there. They were playing the Orioles—Renee's team from when she lived in Maryland, and Cap had taken them to summer games against the Senators. Our seats were way up high behind home plate. This flaming jackass sat directly behind us, guzzling twelve-dollar beers and screaming at the players far below like he knew each one of them personally, and they could hear him and do his bidding. He called them *baby*, and *sweetness* and *honey*, chattered between pitches. "*Ba-ha-ha-ha-ha-ha*," he said. "*Ba-ha-ha-ha-ha, hum babe*."

He was right behind us, this jackass. Him and his girlfriend.

"*Hum babe, it's all you*," he screamed.

It was maybe the fifth inning, Tampa putting it to Baltimore, a good game with lots of hits and foul balls, though a net kept them from falling our way. We'd forgot gloves, me and Lara. She'd grown up watching the World Series every October of her life, and I guess it took. She loved the game, kept stacks of cards and stats. I'd bought her the *Encyclopedia of Baseball,* which was thick as two bricks, and we'd found my uncle Chester in there, who'd once pitched for a Cardinals farm team.

"Trust the Buffalo," the guy hollered. He made a sound I took to be a buffalo, and Renee turned around and glared. He pursed his lips, bellowed.

I said, "Will you please shut up?"

Beside me, Lara said "*Dad*." It was our first time to the majors, after nineteen years of TV ball. I'd promised to take her to the World Series someday. Cap had bought the tickets, and had planned on coming himself, until he learned Renee'd booked a hotel for the night because she knew we'd be drinking, and didn't want to chance driving home, end up on Sheriff's Farm.

"Dude," this guy said, a hurt look on his face. "Trust the Buffalo." He held his plastic stein of beer out for a second.

On the field, the batter'd hit into a double play, everyone around us clapping. Lara stood. She said, *yay*, looked me in the eye.

I said. "Sure. Trust the Buffalo." Then we cheered, rooted for the home team. That night, by the pool, we ate the hotel's free hamburger sliders and all you can drink wine happy hour, and earned our right to the hotel booking. It was hot as hell poolside, and the wine was going down. There was still the threat of the Zika virus, and a whole troupe of house apes were cannonballing the shallow end by our table. But every time the water flew and we were about to say something rude, Lara'd call out, "*Dude.*"

We'd laugh, refill, trust the buffalo.

Renee's brother Rocky'd mapped out a return drive that would take us into what he said was the real Florida, the spine of the state, he called it. Rocky was always trying to show us the authentic Florida. He'd once driven us to a place called Honest John's, a five-hundred-acre compound adjoining a series of barrier islands, where folk motored out in cabin cruisers to get drunk and picnic and shit in the bushes wherever they liked, fly the stars and bars from their mast, fire off pistols if they liked—Honest John was the law at Honest John's. Now he had us headed south and east on roads through sloughs and garden stand towns like Ft. Lonesome and Yee Haw, ripe produce for sale on folding tables. Lara talked Renee into letting her drive the new rental. Only, there'd been a wrong turn. Rocky's Atlas seemed out of scale, so it took five minutes to drive four inches of map, and then we'd hit an intersection where he said go straight, only there was no straight.

From the backseat, Renee barked turns, speed limit, how to adjust the steering wheel. We'd spaced gas. I told her to trust the buffalo, and we rolled into real Florida with a quarter tank.

There were mines.

Rock had said we'd see them, and he knew that where we lived in Utah was the Rio Tinto pit copper mine, largest man-made hole on earth, you could see it from space and off our front porch. He knew it turned my stomach. I'd showed him and told him so the year he and his flame thrower wife'd flown out to ski, only she'd dislocated her shoulder and had to have surgery when they got home, and always blamed it on us. In real Florida, we'd see the mines.

The arms of a train trestle crossing were down, red lights flashing, and a man in a yellow pickup with tires fitted for the tracks waved us through. "Go ahead," he said.

But the arms were down, a bell dinging.

"Lara," Renee said. "He's waving you through. *Go.*"

I said, "Stop."

Lara stopped square on the tracks, right at the high place in the crossing. And at that second, on the tracks, before we drove on, the three of us saw the first of the mines, the land stripped of everything far as you could see. A giant truck with a house sized shovel on front was giving it hell, what in the world? Out there—wasteland, twenty miles or so, six inches of Atlas, moonscape. It was hard to look at, real Florida.

I turned on the radio.

Lara turned it off.

I said, "It's Tom Petty."

She said, "It's *always* Tom Petty."

Renee said, "We need to find a gas station."

"Maybe we'll run out," I said. "Gators'll eat us."

Lara gripped the wheel. Her hands were white. She was a good driver, didn't speed or pass on the right side like Renee had all the way to Tampa. "What's the next town, Dad?"

We passed a mine that had been deserted, its open pit a blue hole now, like back home where kids were always drinking purple Jesus and drowning. "Fort Mead."

"How far?"

"Three inches," I said.

Renee said, "I have to pee. I've had to pee since we left."

Fort Meade was military, this huge funeral home on one side of town, a bridge over the Peace River on the other. Lara checked the oil while I pumped gas and Renee peed. Inside smelled of incense, an Indian man with a statue of Ganesh beside the register.

"Why do they call the river that? Peace?" I asked while he ran my card.

Just then Renee walked out, wiping her hands on her pants. She eyed a stand of watermelon, beefsteak tomatoes and cantaloupe.

He didn't answer, the Indian man. He just smiled, handed me my card, said, "Receipt?"

Outside, Lara squeegeed bugs off the windshield, little squeaks with each stroke. "Let's go home," Lara said.

"The bathroom had a hole in the ceiling. I could see blue sky." Renee had bought a yellow melon, a *Canary* it was called.

That night Rocky served us lobster grilled in buttered foil, filet mignon and green beans, a whole slew of zucchini and key lime pie. We cut the melon. Cap had said the prayer at the end of a makeshift table. He prayed for the sick, the destitute, the infirm and mentally ill. It was the first time we'd all eaten together at Rocky's house since before the divorce, since Meg's death, a good thing, it felt like family. His new wife's teenage daughter was there, her hair dyed coal black. Ray Ray and Angel, they poked their cells.

"Did you see the mines?" Rocky asked.

Lara flashed her eyes.

Back home we argued.

At the big glass table, I'd made a comment about the cat having fleas, how giant cockroaches had attacked Lara that first night. We got into it about the house Rose now co-owned, how it was wood frame instead of steel, not even close to code for a hurricane. No one would ever buy.

"Why do you say that, Joey?" Rose said. She tried to smile.

"I've worked on it twenty years. There's wood rot."

She shook her head. Renee gave me the look. What we were talking about was Captain Rockerson, who he belonged to now.

"How's that?"

I said, "Look at the fascia. Under the cornice."

She said, "Rock?"

"There's a few places," he said. He poured out Bailey's, passed it around.

Rose said, "Stucco. That's what we do in Florida. We don't like something, we stucco it." She smiled, shook her head, walked across the big living room where the light shone on her and Lara, the hair falling on their shoulders, into the master bedroom, where she shut the door, and later we heard them arguing. Her and Cap. She'd taken care of him when he was down, nursed him to health and spent many a night in his hospital room doing so. And there was love. Who can explain that, love?

"You were rude," Renee said.

We were in the guest room where I'd gotten the phone call that my mother had drowned in faraway Arkansas, a decade ago, another world. I said, "I'm sorry."

"You should be. I'm here now. For a reason. Give me that. Stop."

She'd opened the accordion doors to a closet that stretched the width of the far wall. There, her mother's missing paintings, sheet music—Chopin and Stravinsky, the score for Firebird, the leather-bound books of photographs form all the Rockerson's days as a family, back to the wedding in Philipi, Cap in his officer whites, Meg in the flowing bridal gown white as Utah snow. There were photographs of us in there, our wedding, Lara. The smiles on our faces. Moon, our first dog, ten years dead. She'd dug a hole in Meg's flower garden, *Ask Us About Our Grand Dog*, the resulting bumper sticker said.

Cap's Navy sword leaned in its scabbard. She unsheathed it, swished it through the air a few times, then put it back, shut the door, cut the window unit onto high.

In bed, she said, "Goodnight."

The moon was full—light poured through the blinds. Outside, the sprinklers came on. Twenty-some years we'd been coming here. On the night the call came about Mama, Cap had knocked on the door, and I remember the sound of his feet on the tile as he walked away. A full moon night in June, his birthday weekend. Forever, I'd mix them up, *birthday, death day.*

Sunday morning we dressed for church, drove up Oak to St. Sebastian's by the Sea, where Meg's ashes had been deposited in the courtyard, only Cap hadn't marked the spot, so Renee had to guess again, her lips moving, talking to her mother. The grass was thick and green and there was the whiff of ocean, heat coming on already. Organ music came from Sanctuary Hall. Lara wore a pink dress—she was nineteen, beginning her adult life. Renee was here for Cap—she'd grown up Sundays in church, The Nicene Creed and Eucharistic Prayer, the Exchange of Peace.

Across the street was the ballpark, Doug Flutie Field, then the dunes and ocean where Ponce de Leon was rumored to have landed, in search of gold and the fountain of youth.

The program said Eighth Sunday After Pentecost, 2017. We took a pew on the right side—splashed with light from the stained glass—Lara then Renee, me, Rose and Cap. High beyond the altar, a gold plated Bible was opened to Romans 8: 38-39, the reading of the day:

For I am persuaded that neither death nor life, nor angels, nor principalities nor powers, nor things present, nor things to come, nor height, nor depth, nor any other creature shall be able to separate us from the love of God, which is in Christ Jesus, our Lord.

And above this, high beneath the hardwood rafters, the stained-glass portrait for which the church was named, a man shot through with arrows, the grimace of agony fused with tranquility in death. St. Sebastian at the moment the Roman soldiers walked away to the rest of their days and lives, the guilt of having executed one of their own hard on them.

Father Garry was the only person of color in the house, so I could not help seeing him in his pew on the other side, smiling brightly, two weeks from his ordination, the program said. The theme was to be tropical, welcome to Florida, so the congregation was instructed to wear their most colorful, tropical clothes. Around him sat the elderly and afflicted, the limping and halted, fifty or so souls not far from the grave. We were the youngest by decades, save Father Garry, the new shepherd.

We stood for the speaking of the Nicene Creed. Renee spoke by heart, Cap and Rose, the words from their mouths joining with the others, a flash through the brilliant red glass high above the far altar, Sebastian, nude to the waist, tranquil in his agony, a man whose flesh was said to inspire lust, his beauty breathtaking.

It was a woman named Irene, a widower, who'd retrieved the body, and to her shock it lived, this Roman Captain who'd masked his religion, whose face was as handsome as a girl's, he lived.

We look for the resurrection of the dead, all of us said, and I could hear it in Cap's voice, Rose's, Renee's, *and the life of the world to come.*

In three days they'd drive north, the Rockersons, our Lara, Rocky's two teens. They'd ride the autotrain through Virginia, take a driving tour of D.C. He'd show them the Lincoln Memorial where he'd proposed to Meg. They'd circle the beltway, find their old house, traipse over the graves of pets to the ravine where Renee'd once gashed a knee. Back at the hotel, Lara'd call, she'd be sitting outside the hotel door for the quiet. "Mom?" her message would say, "It's raining cats and dogs. Poppy's a bad driver. Is anyone home?"

She'd nursed him, Irene, I don't know how long, the story doesn't say, except that he recovered fully, his vigor resurrected, Sebastian's, in the house of Irene.

Rose turned to me and hesitated, like Poppy had when we'd walked in at sunrise. "Peace be with you," she said. In church, time could hold still, there was prayer, and all those words. She held out her hand, and I took it. We met eyes.

I said, "Peace be with you," turned to my wife and daughter, repeated the words everyone was saying.

After D.C., they'd head north and east over the Chesapeake to New Jersey, and Plainfield. There, in what had once been countryside, sat the old farmhouse where Cap had been born, the sweeping front porch wrapping around the corner to the pool which had been filled in and now sat in shadow. He'd find a plastic tag with number ten on it from a cow he himself had cared for when he was her age, Lara'd say, before the Navy and War College, and all the rest. They'd walk right up on the front porch of the now vacant house and be photographed together, Poppy and Lara. It was emotional, she'd say.

Irene could not stop him from returning to Rome to preach the Gospel, even to the magistrate who'd sent him to death the first time, or so he believed, but she must have tried. Surely she tried. Captain of the Praetorian Guard, Officer in the Army of Rome, liege to the Emperor, proud stubborn man with his clean-shaven face and boyish smile, his voice as tender as a girl's. Had she professed love, his nurse, Irene? Who was this god to demand a second martyrdom? And after it was done—as it surely would be—would she seek his corpse a second time? Had he looked back at her from the hill's rise, the sunlight shining on her hair? By some accounts he was beheaded, the body thrown into a common sewer. A cult of Sebastian grew, the paintings, he was said to reappear at times, to have interceded for those stricken by the Black Plague. His cranium came to a town in Germany, a Benedictine Abbey where they drank wine from the silver encased skull on his feast day. *Santa Meurte*, the Spanish called him, Saint of Death.

I had long mistaken the stained glass rendering as the crucified Christ, not knowing that the town of Sebastian twenty miles south and Sebastian Inlet and the freshwater Saint Sebastian River which flowed into the sea, were all markers of the cult that had flourished here. After the twelve Spanish galleons heavy-loaded with pieces of eight were blown off course by a hurricane, the surviving seamen had swum aground and prayed to him, Sebastian, who hung on the gorgeously stained column above me, my daughter and wife. There as we took the host between our lips that last Sunday morning with Poppy not far from where the saint of death was said to have walked from the water nude and shining and gloriously alive.

Lara would not tell us about the vulture until some weeks later, and even then as an aside, a strange confession that would color her face. Before they had left Cummings Road and all the Rockerson farmhouse had stood for across the generations, Poppy walked one last time into the derelict barn with its broken tools and six-toed cats. Lara went with him, Rose in the car now, ready to roll, put this chapter behind them for good and ever and get on with life. Rocky's kids, Ray and Angel, they walked in too, the cool and shadowy space reeking of mold and shit from long dead animals. The four held hands in the dark. The barn was old. It no longer mattered. Through a wall visible by the open manger, they heard the sound of something living, large enough to rattle boards, the beat of wings, it sounded like, a leaping and falling. There was something alive in there, a soft cry, recognizable though strange. They saw it in a shaft of light, through the manger the four made witness: "It was an eagle, daddy, I mean a vulture. It was a vulture living in Poppy's barn."

Santa Meurte gleaming behind our backs, we walked out the cast open double doors, shook Father Garry's hand and walked past the piece of grassy earth that was Meg's grave. A soft rain fell that afternoon, and Lara and I went out on bicycles, found the Indian River's wooded path to a park of twisted trees. There was a fountain there, no one to drink but me and her.

"Maybe this is it," I said, the drapes parting then closing on a house across the street. She said, "May be," and we drank long of the cool, clean water.

The next morning before sunrise, before departure, the three of us would rise early and walk east to the beach access, the world quiet with the smell of blooming flowers and ocean. A white tanker sailed the far blue curve of ocean. Stiff wind in our faces, we'd go barefoot down the dune, trace unmolested turtle tracks to the breakers. They'd meet us there, the elderly, a whole troop of them in birthday suits out for morning exercise. Their sex faded, how they flapped their shadow wings, very much alive, blood rising from the heart root. The last of the moon on their skins, they'd tightrope the seam between sea foam and earth, engulfed in the alpenglow of new-risen sun. Naked souls, they'd turn into the sea, arms thrown wide for the embrace.